Maggie bristled.
"My sister didn't take her life."

Nate glanced down at his notes. "Let's go back to the beginning. What happened after you entered the house?"

She explained how she had searched the rooms and, finding nothing, had made her way to the attic. "The upstairs was pitch-black. I couldn't see anything and waved my hand in the air to find the pull cord for the overhead light bulb. The moon shone through the window and−" She struggled to find her words.

His voice softened. "That's when you saw your sister?"

She nodded. Tears pooled in her blue-green eyes and slowly trickled down her cheeks. Nate pulled his handkerchief from his pocket and shoved it into her hand, his fingers touching hers for longer than necessary.

Maggie seemed oblivious to the way his hand burned where it touched hers. What was happening to his ability to remain neutral? No one had ever affected him like the woman sitting close to him.

Books by Debby Giusti

Love Inspired Suspense

Nowhere to Hide
Scared to Death
MIA: Missing in Atlanta
*Countdown to Death
*Protecting Her Child
Christmas Peril
  "Yule Die"
Killer Headline
†The Officer's Secret

*Magnolia Medical
†Military Investigations

DEBBY GIUSTI

is a medical technologist who loves working with test tubes and petri dishes almost as much as she loves to write. Growing up as an army brat, Debby met and married her husband—then a captain in the army—at Fort Knox, Kentucky. Together they traveled the world, raised three wonderful army brats of their own and have now settled in Atlanta, Georgia, where Debby spins tales of suspense that touch the heart and soul. Contact Debby through her website, www.DebbyGiusti.com, email debby@debbygiusti.com, or write c/o Love Inspired Suspense, 233 Broadway, Suite 1001, New York, NY 10279.

The Officer's Secret
Secret

Debby Giusti

Love Inspired

Recycling programs
for this product may
not exist in your area.

™ LOVE INSPIRED BOOKS

ISBN-13: 978-0-373-44442-7

THE OFFICER'S SECRET

www.LoveInspiredBooks.com

Printed in U.S.A.

If you remain in my word,
you will truly be my disciples, and you will
know the truth, and the truth will set you free.
—*John* 8:31, 32

To Tony and Joseph
My Military Heroes

To our brave men and women in uniform
God bless you

and

God bless the United States of America

To the Seekers
Thanks for making it so much fun!

To my editor, Emily Rodmell
You always make my stories better

To Tony, Liz, Eric, Mary, Katie and Joe
To Anna, Robert, John Anthony and baby William
I love you all so much!

PROLOGUE

The night lay cold and dark outside the car just like the layer of regret that hung around Maggie Bennett's heart. She had left Fort Rickman as a young teen, vowing never to return. Too many painful memories were associated with the army post, memories Maggie had secreted away in the deepest recesses of her heart. Tonight, she prayed those memories would remain hidden forever.

Squinting through the rain-spattered windshield, she approached Fort Rickman's main gate and parked in front of the Visitor's Center. The clock on the dashboard read 2:15 a.m., a chilling reminder of the urgency of the middle-of-the-night plea that brought her here.

If not for her sister's phone call, Maggie would still be sound asleep at home in Alabama instead of seeking entry to the Georgia army post she had left sixteen years ago. Dani's attempt at reconciliation last week when the two sisters had met for lunch had been as unexpected after their years of separation as tonight's phone call. Maggie had been surprised that Dani would reach out to her so soon after opening up communication again, but she wasn't going to let her sister down. Not this time.

With a heavy sigh, she pulled her key from the ignition and stepped from her car, shivering, not so much from the cold February night air but in anticipation of what awaited her. Perhaps Dani's outreach would move them beyond the pain of their estrangement.

How had the years passed without either of them making an effort to reconnect? After more than a decade of silence, her sister's invitation to meet for lunch had been a welcome first step. Both of them had been guarded at the onset. Then slowly, recalling their childhood days, the sibling bond had semisurfaced and opened them to share at least a bit more deeply.

Maggie had known intuitively that Dani had changed, even before she had mentioned her time in Afghanistan. The deployment had provided an opportunity for her sister to reflect on the purpose of her life and, as she had told Maggie, she'd eventually realized her marriage to Graham had been a huge mistake. As soon as Dani had returned to the States, she had tried to explain to her husband the way she felt, but he hadn't wanted to listen. Evidently Dani had been more insistent tonight.

Over lunch, Dani had also alluded to a possible illegal operation she had uncovered during her deployment, something that could put her in danger if the wrong people found out. She hadn't divulged any of the details to Maggie, although she had voiced her own hesitation about telling Graham. He traveled to the Middle East with the civilian contracting job he had on post, and for a reason her sister never divulged, Dani felt she couldn't confide in him—nor could she confide in the military police on post, who Dani believed could in some way be connected to the Afghani operation. All of which made Maggie wonder whether her sister thought Graham was involved, as well.

The old Dani never worried about the future, but

Maggie had heard concern in her sister's voice a week ago and had seen the glint of fear in her eyes, no matter how hard Dani had tried to cover her anxiety with a nervous laugh.

Neither sibling had mentioned their father's death or leaving Fort Rickman years earlier, yet the topic had hovered like a dark cloud over their time together until, in parting, Dani had opened her arms and the two women had embraced, both with some hesitation and neither making the most of the moment. Yet the outreach on Dani's part had been significant enough to, if not knit the tear, at least bandage the wound she doubted would ever completely heal.

Pushing aside the guilt that had claimed her heart for too long, Maggie tugged her coat closed against the wind and hurried inside where the glare of fluorescent lights greeted her along with the brisk "Welcome to Fort Rickman" of the military policeman on duty.

With a perfunctory nod, she pulled her driver's license and registration form from her purse. After giving him the documents, she raked her free hand through her chestnut-colored hair, painfully aware of her disheveled appearance.

If only she had changed into something more presentable than faded jeans and a baggy orange sweater prior to starting out on her journey. As distraught as Dani had sounded over the phone, Maggie's focus had been on packing a suitcase and heading for the highway. She'd made the trip in a little over two hours.

"Ma'am, your reason for entering post?"

The MP's question brought to mind a number of answers. "I'm here to see my sister, Major Danielle Bennett. She lives at Quarters 1448 Hunter Road."

Referencing Maggie's license and registration form, he typed information into a computer database before he handed them back to her along with the visitor's pass. After a hasty word of thanks, Maggie scurried to her car, threw the pass onto the dashboard and climbed behind the wheel. A sense of déjà vu, mixed with sadness, slipped around her shoulders as she drove through the main gate and entered post.

Maggie passed the Post Exchange and Commissary and caught sight of the old movie theater in the distance. All too vividly, she remembered sitting by herself, while a few rows over, Dani watched the movie surrounded by friends—mainly boys taken with her raven hair and rounded curves. As a young teen, Maggie had been bashful, gawky and underdeveloped.

Uncomfortable dwelling on the reality of her childhood, she refocused her eyes on the road ahead. Speed limit thirty miles per hour, a road sign warned. Maggie checked her speedometer. Easing up on the accelerator, she made the first of a series of turns that eventually led to the old housing area where brick homes sat guarded by stately oaks. She entered the subdivision painfully aware of even more memories that bubbled up from her youth. Despite the years that had passed, the streets were still familiar. Maggie turned right at the first intersection and pulled to a stop in front of Quarters 1448 where her sister now lived.

For a long moment, she stared at the Federalist-style structure built in the early 1900s, knowing farther down the road and on the opposite side of the street sat another two-story house with the identical floor plan where Dani and Maggie and their parents had lived when the girls were teens. Their dad's assignment had been cut short by his death—a tragedy that haunted her still. Dani carried the guilt on her shoulders, while Maggie carried it in her heart.

Pulling in a calming breath and forcing her mind back to the problem at hand, she yanked the keys from the ignition, grabbed her purse and overnight bag and stepped onto the sidewalk. This wasn't the time to revisit the past.

Maggie needed to focus on her sister's problems. Dani's voice had been stretched thin over the phone when she'd called, and the nervous laughter Maggie had heard at lunch last week had been replaced with labored pulls of air brimming with tension. The fact that Dani had even called made Maggie realize how desperate her sister was for help.

Graham had moved out a week ago, but he kept coming back, insisting their marriage could be saved. Finally, Dani had told him point-blank she wanted a divorce. Never one to be pushed around, Graham had balked at first until he finally realized Dani wouldn't change her mind.

The Graham Hughes Maggie remembered usually got what he wanted. And from what Dani had said, it sounded as if Graham wanted his marriage intact, which was why Maggie had packed a suitcase and driven two hours to arrive at Fort Rickman in the middle of the night. Not that Maggie could provide protection, but she could offer her sister much-needed support.

Before closing the driver's door, she dug into her handbag for the house key Dani had insisted she take when they'd finished their lunch last week and were ready to part company again.

"Just in case," she'd said, giving no other information

as she had shoved the key into Maggie's hand. Now glad of her sister's forethought, Maggie climbed the steps to the front porch and knocked repeatedly on the door. When no one answered, she slid the key into the lock and stepped inside, feeling an immediate sense of coming home.

Her gaze swept Dani's living room, taking in the two Queen Anne chairs, the couch and love seat and then the marble-topped coffee table decorated with memorabilia her sister had kept that honored their military dad. His medals and the flag that had draped his coffin were both displayed in glass cases, reminders of the man he once had been.

Leaving her suitcase and purse in the foyer, Maggie shrugged out of her coat and followed a lone light into the kitchen. Neat, uncluttered, every item in its place and, just as with the living room, so like their house of old. Their mother had been a meticulous housekeeper, and from the looks of Dani's quarters, she kept her own house as tidy as their mother had up until her own death years ago.

Circling through the dining area, Maggie stopped at the foot of the stairs. She glanced up and listened, hearing nothing except the wind buffeting the house.

"Dani?" On the phone her sister had mentioned being tired. Had she gone to bed?

Maggie flipped on the upper hall light and climbed the wooden stairway that wound to the second story. A small bathroom sat at the top of the landing, flanked by two bedrooms. Searching for her sister, she glanced into each room—one of which had been turned into an office—before she headed for the master suite and tapped on the door.

Stepping into the darkened interior, Maggie switched on the lamp, noting the neatly made bed and undisturbed accent pillows. The bath and dressing area beyond sat vacant, as well. Backtracking to the head of the stairs, she peered over the banister, debating her options, then refocused her gaze on the closed door at the end of the hallway.

Her pulse quickened, pounding against the tendons in her neck, filling her ears with the thump of her own heartbeat. Visions from the past returned to taunt her as they often did in the stillness of the night.

Her father's body shrouded in death.

Her mother's screams of disbelief.

Maggie shook her head ever so slightly, scattering the memories that clouded her consciousness.

"Let the dead bury the dead," came the words from scripture. Maggie had moved on with her life and didn't need reminders to draw her back in time.

What about Dani?

Over lunch and again on the phone tonight, she had sidestepped mention of their father's death. The realization that Dani could still be caught in the past unnerved Maggie. With purposeful steps, she walked to the end of the hallway. The stairs to the attic sat behind the closed door. Maggie grabbed the knob and tugged it open.

Light from the hall spilled across the bottom steps. Pulling in a fortifying breath, she climbed the stairs, one foot after the other. At the top, she peered into the darkness and swatted the air, hoping to make contact with a pull string for the overhead light just as she had done years ago in her childhood quarters.

A sound below punctuated the stillness. Footsteps or the creaks of an aged house? Perhaps Dani was home after all. Maggie turned to descend the stairs she had just climbed.

A moonbeam broke through the dormer window, cascading light into the corner of the attic where an overturned ladder-back chair lay on the floor.

The hair on the back of her neck rose in protest.

"No!" Maggie screamed as she raised her eyes and focused on her sister's body, hanging from the rafters.

ONE

Chief Warrant Officer Nathaniel Patterson, U.S. Army Criminal Investigation Division, got the call at 0315. *Possible suicide at Quarters 1448 Hunter Road.*

Arriving fifteen minutes later, he parked behind two MP sedans and stepped from his car, adjusting his weapon on his hip. Although Nate hadn't known Major Bennett, the death of an officer was significant, and tonight, the combined resources of the military police and the army's major crime unit, the CID, had been called in to investigate the case.

Headlights signaled an approaching vehicle. Nate waited as his friend and fellow agent, Jamison Steele, crawled from his late-model sports car. Dressed in a tweed sports coat and gray trousers, he looked like a fashionable young executive in contrast to Nate's run-of-the-mill navy blazer and khaki slacks.

With a hasty nod, Jamison fell into step beside Nate and followed him up the front steps in silence. Before either man could knock, Corporal Robert Mills opened the door. The young MP had the makings of a future CID special agent if he learned to keep his somewhat self-centered ego in check. Nate chalked it up to youth.

Hopefully over time, his impetuous nature would mellow.

Raising his right hand to his forehead, Mills saluted the two warrant officers. "Evening, Mr. Patterson. Mr. Steele."

The agents returned the salute and stepped into the brightly lit foyer. Nate glanced into the living room where a woman sat huddled in a high-backed chair. Blue-green eyes looked up with the hollow stare of shock he'd seen too many times at crime scenes. The raw emotion written so clearly on her face brought home the tragic reality of what had happened tonight.

Their eyes met and held for an instant, causing an unexpected warmth to curl through Nate's gut. Then, tugging on a strand of her auburn hair, she dropped her gaze, breaking their momentary connection and leaving Nate with an emptiness he couldn't explain. Probably the middle-of-the-night phone call and his attempt to respond as quickly as possible that had thrown him slightly out of sync.

Or maybe it was the woman—a family member, perhaps.

Putting a human face on the tragedy—a very pretty face—intensified his desire to learn the truth about what had happened tonight. Nate was good at what he did. Tonight he wanted to be even better. The woman deserved as much. So did the victim waiting for him upstairs.

Bottom line, the army took care of its own in life and especially so in death. He motioned Corporal Mills into the kitchen as Jamison headed upstairs. Nate pulled out a small notebook and ballpoint pen from his breast pocket then, lowering his voice, he nodded toward the living room. "So who's the woman?"

"She's the sister of the deceased, sir. Name's Margaret Bennett, but she goes by Maggie. She found the major's body in the attic."

Nate knew how tough it was to lose a sibling. He thought of his own brother. Although eight years had separated them in age, they'd always been close.

He scribbled Maggie's name on a blank page of his notebook. "Apparent suicide?"

"Roger that, sir. Major Bennett hung herself from a rafter. Sergeant Thorndike's upstairs. He wanted me to check for prints."

A half-empty bottle of cabernet sat on the counter. Nate pointed to a wineglass, stained with residue. "Be sure to send off a toxicology sample on whatever's in the bottom of that glass."

"Yes, sir."

Opening the dishwasher, Nate used a latex glove he pulled from his pocket and lifted a second wineglass onto the counter. "Check the bottle and both glasses for prints. Let me know what you find."

"Will do, sir."

Nate nodded his thanks to Mills, returned the notebook to his pocket and grabbed a water glass from the cabinet, which he filled from the tap. Leaving the kitchen, he approached the woman in the living room.

"Excuse me, ma'am. I thought you might be thirsty."

Maggie Bennett glanced up with tear-filled eyes and a drawn face that expressed the heartbreak of a deeply personal loss. The two sisters must have been close. His heart went out to her, understanding all too well the pain she must be feeling.

"I'm Special Agent Nate Patterson, U.S. Army Criminal Investigation Division." With his free hand, he pulled out his CID identification, although he doubted Ms. Bennett would question his credentials. At the moment, she looked like a frightened stray caught in a trap. A beautiful stray, he decided, noting her high cheekbones, arched brows and full lips. But her strikingly good looks were overshadowed by a blanket of grief that lay like a black veil over her alabaster skin.

"I'm the lead investigator on this case, ma'am. Please accept my condolences as well as the heartfelt sympathy of the CID and the Military Police Corps here at Fort Rickman."

She bit her lip, then mumbled a broken, "Thank… thank you."

"I'll be upstairs for a few minutes. When I return I'd like to talk to you about your sister." He placed the water on the end table.

She gave a brief, pained smile of thanks at the offered glass and then looked back at him. "Yes, of course. Whatever you need to know."

Nate climbed the stairs to the second floor, feeling the weight of Maggie's grief resting on his shoulders. He'd give her a few minutes to gather strength before he saddled her with the endless questions that any death investigation required.

Reaching the second landing, Nate glanced into the home office on the right where Corporal Raynard Otis attempted to access the victim's laptop computer files. The soldier looked up, a full smile spreading across his honey-brown face. "Hey, sir. How's it going?"

"You tell me, Ray."

"Should have something for you shortly."

"That's what I like to hear."

Nate continued on to the open attic door. Rapid flashes of light confirmed the military photographer was already on the job. Within the hour, photos would appear on Nate's computer, systematically capturing every detail of the attic scene.

On the opposite side of the hallway, Jamison questioned a military policewoman and jotted down pertinent information she shared, information the CID team would review over and over again until all the facts were in and a determination could be made about the actual cause of death. Foul play needed to be ruled out. Hopefully, the case would be open and shut.

Climbing the stairs to the attic, Nate eyed the rafter and the thick hemp rope wrapped around the sturdy crossbeam. Without forethought, he touched his breast pocket where he had tucked the notebook, containing Maggie's name, as if to shield her from the grim reality of her sister's death. Lowering his gaze, he took in the victim's black hair and swollen face.

God rest her soul. The prayer surfaced from his past. His mother's influence, no doubt. She had raised him to be a believer, although his faith had never been strong, and for the past eight months, he had tuned God out of his life completely.

Once again, his hand sought the notebook as his eyes refocused on the body.

Death by strangulation was never pretty, yet despite the victim's contorted features, he recognized the same classic beauty that the very much alive sister sitting downstairs possessed. The deceased, with her low-cut silk blouse and snug-fitting leggings, appeared to be the more flamboyant sibling in contrast to Maggie's modest jeans and sweater, but appearances could lie, and more than anything else, Nate needed the truth.

A chair lay at Major Bennett's feet. Classic suicide scenario. In all probability, the victim had stood on the chair to secure the rope around the crossbeam and the noose around her neck. Kicking over the chair would leave her hanging and preclude the major from saving herself, should she have second thoughts about taking her own life.

Staff Sergeant Larry Thorndike stepped forward. The military policeman was mid-fifties with a receding hairline and an extra twenty pounds of weight around his middle.

"The victim worked in Headquarters Company of the 2nd Transportation Battalion," Staff Sergeant Thorndike offered as Nate glanced his way. "The major redeployed home from Afghanistan fourteen days ago as part of the advance party."

"Same unit that had two casualties in Afghanistan this week?" Nate asked.

"That's right, sir. Captain York—the company commander—and his driver hit an improvised explosive device. Now this. It's hard on the unit. Hard on everyone."

Nate knew all too well the tragic consequences an IED could cause. Was that what had led to the major's suicide? Had she felt in any way responsible for the captain's death? "How long before the medical examiner gets here?"

"The ME should be here any minute."

"Did you talk to the sister?"

The sergeant nodded. "But only briefly. She's pretty shook up."

An understatement from what Nate had seen.

"Ms. Bennett had enough sense to call for help," Sergeant Thorndike continued. "When I arrived she was white as a sheet and hyperventilating. Said she lives in Independence, Alabama. Received a phone call at approximately 2330 hours from the deceased. The victim sounded anxious, according to the sister. Major Bennett had fought with her estranged husband, Graham Hughes, shortly before the phone call."

"The major used her maiden name?"

"Roger that, sir."

"Has the husband been notified?"

"Negative. We're trying to track him down. Evidently he moved out a few days after Major Bennett arrived stateside."

"Alert the post chaplain to a possible notification of next of kin. I'll want to talk to the husband. Let me know when you find out where he's staying."

"Will do, sir." The sergeant unclipped his cell phone from his belt and stepped to the corner of the attic to call the chaplain.

Nate neared the body. He examined the knots that formed the noose and then the victim's neck and hands, noting her intact skin. No signs of struggle. Blood had pooled in her extremities, consistent with death by hanging and the beginnings of rigor mortis. It all looked like a textbook suicide, and yet... Something about it bothered him, and it took a minute to put his finger on it.

The sergeant closed his cell. "Chaplain Grant will be here shortly, sir."

Nate pointed to the victim's bare feet. "Where are her shoes?"

"Main floor, sir. Under a table by the door."

"It's a cold night. Why would Major Bennett walk around her house without shoes?"

The sergeant shrugged. "You got me there, sir."

Footsteps sounded on the stairs. Nate turned as Major Brett Hansen, the pathologist and medical examiner on post stepped into the attic. "Good to see you, Nate."

"Sir."

The major nodded to the sergeant and photographer. "What do we have here, gentlemen?"

Nate filled him in on the somewhat limited information accumulated so far. Wasting no time, the doc slipped on latex gloves and began his visual exam of the victim's body. Once complete, Sergeant Thorndike would lower her to the floor so additional forensic evidence could be gathered.

Knowing the procedure would take time, Nate descended the stairs to the first floor where the bereaved sister sat, legs crossed and head resting in her hands.

Peering into the kitchen, he saw Mills bent over the wine bottle. "Find anything yet?"

The MP looked up. "The glass you pulled from the dishwasher had been wiped clean, sir. We might get lucky on the bottle."

"Good man."

Entering the living room, Nate glanced, once again, at the grief-stricken woman. She appeared fragile as a butterfly and, no doubt, was devastated by what she'd discovered tonight. As much as he hated to disturb her, Nate needed information.

Moving closer, he touched her shoulder. The knit of

her sweater was soft to his fingertips. "Ms. Bennett? Maggie?"

She looked up, startled. The pain in her eyes cut through him like a well-aimed laser beam.

"If I could have a few minutes of your time, ma'am."

Fatigue lined her oval face, but her ashen coloring concerned him more. She had found her sister's body and was surrounded by law enforcement personnel trying to make sense of a tragic death. No one had time to offer her more than a perfunctory word of compassion or support.

He glanced at the empty glass on the end table. "Would you like more water?"

She shook her head and rubbed her hands over her arms. "Thank you, no."

"If you're cold, I could raise the thermostat?"

"I…I'm just tired."

"Of course." He pulled up a chair. "Could you tell me what happened tonight?"

When she didn't answer, he scooted closer. "I know it's difficult."

She nodded. "Dani called me. She was upset… almost hysterical. She had told her husband she wanted a divorce."

Nate removed the notebook and pen from his pocket. He needed to put aside the fact that this woman ignited a spark of interest deep within him and focus instead on the questions he had to ask and she, hopefully, would be able to answer.

"Graham…" Maggie hesitated. "My sister's husband wanted them to reconcile."

"Go on." Painfully aware of the heat that continued

to warm his gut, Nate swallowed hard and concentrated on the information Maggie began to recount.

"They…they had argued. Graham was upset. But then so was my sister. Dani told him to leave. Obviously, he… he came back later and—"

When she failed to complete the statement, Nate asked, "When did your sister and Mr. Hughes marry?"

"Dani ran into him shortly after she transferred here to Rickman. That was two years ago. They dated a few months. She sent me a wedding announcement after they were married."

"You attended the ceremony?"

"I wasn't invited."

Could Maggie's dislike of her brother-in-law stem from being excluded from their wedding? Nate drew a question mark on his tablet before asking, "Did you know Graham?"

"Yes."

"Had infidelity been an issue?"

She wiped her hand over her cheek and sniffed. "Not that Dani mentioned. But when we met for lunch last week, she told me that their marriage was over."

Nate nodded as he continued writing. "When you entered the house, did anything indicate Graham *had* been here?"

"A bottle of wine on the kitchen counter. Dani never drank red wine."

"What about her husband?"

"I…I don't know. When I was upstairs, I heard footsteps on the first floor." Maggie bit her lip and shook her head ever so slightly, her eyes widening with realization. "Graham must have been in the house the whole time I was searching for my sister."

"Did you *see* Graham Hughes?"

"No, but it had to be him."

Had to was supposition. Maggie seemed eager to place blame on her brother-in-law's shoulders. Too eager? No matter how unlikely, if Major Bennett's death were ruled a homicide, the beautiful woman sitting next to Nate could end up being a person of interest, as well.

"Was the front door locked when you arrived?"

Maggie nodded. "I knocked. Dani had mentioned being tired. I thought she might be sleeping. When she didn't answer the door, I used the key she had given me when we met for lunch."

"Did your sister say why she wanted you to have a key to her house when you lived so far apart?"

"No, and I didn't ask for an explanation. Dani and I had been estranged for a few years. I was relieved that we were trying to patch up our differences."

"What type of differences?"

She lowered her gaze and uncrossed her legs. Nate watched her body language. Her refusal to make eye contact was telling.

Finally she shrugged and tried to smile. "Two women going their separate ways. Dani went into the military. I pursued a career in family counseling."

Nate was sure there had been more to the *differences* than Maggie was willing to admit. "Did Major Bennett invite you to visit this weekend?"

With a quick shake of her head, she said, "Dani was independent. She had a hard time accepting help."

"Yet—" Nate glanced at the small suitcase in the foyer "—you packed a bag and drove here to be with her."

"I told Dani she shouldn't be alone, that I was worried Graham might come back."

"And Major Bennett shared your concern about her husband?"

"She was more upset about something that had happened in Afghanistan. But she didn't go into the problem. Only that it was serious."

Nate raised his brow. "Serious enough to cause her to take her own life?"

Maggic bristled. "My sister didn't take her life."

Nate wouldn't state the obvious, which was that, at this early stage in the investigation, nothing indicated foul play.

"How long ago did you and your sister reconnect?"

"Dani called last week and asked if we could meet for lunch, which we did, in Alabama."

"Not here on post?"

"That's right. We met just over the state line in a little town called Hope. There's a ladies' tearoom on the square."

Nate would have someone check out the tearoom. Not that he thought Maggic was lying, but he wanted to ensure the information was accurate before he passed it up the chain of command.

"How did your sister seem? Happy? Sad?"

"She was concerned about her marriage, but she wasn't depressed, if that's what you're asking."

"What did you talk about?"

Maggie shrugged. "Her deployment. Being back in the States."

"Her marriage?"

"Yes, of course. She said marrying Graham had been a mistake."

"Did she give a reason?"

Maggie shook her head.

"What about growing up? Did you reminisce about the good times?"

"Sure. We were always close as kids."

"But that changed?" he asked.

"We…we grew apart, as I mentioned."

"Looking back to your childhood, what thoughts come to mind?"

A hint of a smile tugged at Maggie's lips. "Running barefoot in the backyard."

"Sounds as if you and your sister didn't like shoes."

"Only when we were little. Dani had a closet full when we were teens."

"But she went barefoot in the house?"

Maggie wrinkled her brow. "Not that I recall."

Nate glanced down at his notes. "Let's go back to the beginning. What happened after you entered the house?"

She explained how she had searched the rooms and, finding nothing, had made her way to the attic. "The upstairs was pitch-black. I couldn't see anything and waved my hand in the air to find the pull cord for the overhead lightbulb."

"If you hadn't been here before, how did you know about the pull cord?"

Angling her head, she paused, as if weighing her words. "My dad was military," she said at last. "We lived in similar quarters sixteen years ago."

"At Fort Rickman?"

"That's right. In this same housing area."

"A three-year assignment for your dad?"

"Yes, but—"

Maggie clasped her hands then worried her fingers. "My father…" Deep breath. "His tour of duty was cut short." She looked down as if gathering courage to go on. "Regrettably, my father committed suicide."

Not what he had expected to hear. Nate fought to keep his expression neutral as she glanced up at him with troubled eyes.

"He hanged himself in the attic of our house." She leaned closer to Nate. "The similarity in the two deaths proves Dani would never have taken her own life."

"Because—?"

Her eyes widened as if the conclusion she had drawn was obvious. "Because Dani did everything to overcome the stigma of his death. That's why she went into the military. She idolized him. Dani tried to be the son he always wanted. Problem was she tried to prove herself to him, even after his death." She leaned closer. "Don't you see, for Dani, suicide wouldn't have been an option?"

Unless Major Bennett wanted to prove how much she loved her father by following him into death. Nate kept that thought to himself.

"You brought up depression earlier. Is there a history of depression or anxiety disorders in your family?"

"None that I know of."

"Tell me about when you were in the attic. You said the light was off?"

"That's correct. The moon shone through the window and—" She struggled to find her words.

His voice softened. "That's when you saw your sister?"

She nodded. Tears pooled in her blue-green eyes and slowly trickled down her cheeks. Nate tried to remain detached despite his desire to wipe away her pain. He pulled his handkerchief from his pocket and shoved it into her hand, his fingers touching hers for longer than necessary, as if attempting to pass on support.

Maggie seemed oblivious to the way his hand burned where it touched hers. What was happening to his ability to remain neutral? He had been around other attractive women…had dated a few along the way…but no one had ever affected him like the woman sitting close to him.

Nate turned to look over his shoulder as Jamison scurried down the stairs and motioned him into the foyer, providing the reprieve Nate needed. Time to regroup and focus on the internal warning signal that was telling him something unexpected and downright powerful was happening to his status quo.

"Excuse me for a minute." He rose from the chair and met the agent in the kitchen.

"You okay?" Jamison stared at him with narrowed eyes.

Nate straightened his shoulders. "Yeah, why?"

"You look troubled."

"An officer died tonight. That is troubling."

"Of course, it is. The ME is getting ready to release the body. They'll bring Major Bennett downstairs soon. Might not be good for her sister to watch."

Jamison was right. Maggie shouldn't be around when the body was removed.

"What did the doc say?" Nate asked.

"Only that he'll order a toxicology screen. Drugs and alcohol. As backed up as the lab is at Fort Gillem, I don't know when we'll get the results back, though."

"See what you can find out about Major Bennett's father," Nate said. "He was stationed at Rickman sixteen years ago and evidently committed suicide."

Jamison let out a low whistle. "Quite a coincidence."

Before Nate could respond, the front door opened and CID agent Kelly McQueen scurried inside and joined the men in the kitchen. She was blond-haired and blue-eyed and the best marksman in the unit.

"What do you need me to do?" she asked after Nate filled her in on what they had learned so far.

"Help me decide where Major Bennett's sister can stay tonight," Nate said. "The downtown area has had problems with all the rain. The basement of the Freemont Hotel is flooded, and they've shut down temporarily."

A number of small motels were located immediately off post, but most of them were fleabag rentals that catered to a transient troop population. At this difficult time, Maggie deserved something more accommodating.

"I've got an extra room," Kelly volunteered. "She's welcome to stay at my place."

Nate nodded. "That works."

Kelly was good at her job and had compassion to embrace someone reeling with grief. Her apartment was directly across from Nate's in the bachelor officer quarters on post so he would be able to keep an eye on Maggie and offer his support.

"I'll have Mills follow us to the BOQ," said Nate. "He can bring me back here once I get Maggie settled."

The corporal responded with a thumbs-up. "Can do, sir. By the way, Ms. Bennett's driving a silver Saturn. I checked the car and her personal effects. She's clean."

"You need authorization."

Mill's face darkened.

"We'll talk about it tomorrow."

"Yes, sir."

"What about the wine bottle? Did you find prints?"

"Negative."

Nate turned back to Jamison. "Pull the major's medical records and see if there's any history of psychological problems. Also, check with the main gate and find out what time the sister, and any other guests the major may have had this evening, entered post. Question the neighbors in case the major and her husband aired their dirty laundry and find out if any strange cars or visitors stopped by this evening."

"Will do," Jamison said.

"Lieutenant Colonel Foglio lives across the street," Kelly volunteered. "That teenage son of his is staying with his dad again."

"The one with the tattoos?" Jamison asked. "What's his name? Carl, Kurt…?"

"It's Kyle," Kelly said. "After the trouble he got into last summer, I didn't think Lieutenant Colonel Foglio's current wife would allow the kid back in her house."

"Be sure to ask Foglio where his son has been this evening," Nate said to Jamison.

"You got it."

"Have we located Graham Hughes yet?" Nate asked.

Jamison pulled a notebook from his pocket. "I called his boss. Graham's a civilian contractor who works for AmeriWorks. After splitting with his wife, he moved in temporarily with a guy who has the desk next to him in the contracting office. The guy's name is—" Jamison referred to his notes "Arnold Zart. Travels between

Fort Rickman and various forward operating bases in Afghanistan. He's got an apartment off post."

Nate nodded. "Once we get the sister settled in at Kelly's place, the chaplain and I will pay Mr. Zart a visit."

Jamison removed a sheet of paper from his notepad and offered the handwritten note to Nate. "Here's Zart's address."

"Thanks." Nate stepped back into the living room and motioned Kelly forward. "Maggie, this is Special Agent Kelly McQueen." Kelly offered a few words of compassion along with a warm smile.

"Agent McQueen has a spare room at her place," Nate continued. "You'll be able to get some rest there tonight, and we can talk more in the morning."

"But I…" Maggie looked around seemingly momentarily confused.

"I'm going home shortly," Kelly said. "You and Nate can take your time and come over when you're ready."

With a final smile, Kelly headed into the foyer just as the front door opened once again. Chaplain Grant, a tall lieutenant colonel with a sincere face, stepped inside.

Nate excused himself from Maggie and approached the chaplain. "Thanks for being here, sir."

"Terrible shame."

"Yes, sir." Nate lowered his voice. "Major Bennett and her husband had separated about a week ago. He's currently staying with a guy who works with him in the AmeriWorks contracting office on post."

"Over the phone, Sergeant Thorndike mentioned a sister from Alabama."

Nate nodded. "She's had a rough night. The sister's the one who found the major's body." Nate ushered the chaplain toward the living room, introduced him to Maggie and then stepped back, giving the two of them a bit of privacy while the lieutenant colonel offered words of comfort, which Maggie seemed to appreciate.

"Have you talked to your brother-in-law?" the chaplain eventually asked her. When she shook her head, Chaplain Grant turned serious eyes toward Nate. "Might be beneficial to have Maggie with us when we notify Mr. Hughes."

"Ah, sir—?" Before Nate could register an objection to the idea, the chaplain had refocused his gaze on Maggie.

"I'm sure you and Mr. Hughes have things you'd like to discuss, concerning your sister's internment, if you feel up to seeing him at this late hour."

Maggie nodded. "You're right, Chaplain. I…I need to talk to Graham."

Nate wasn't sure whether her current interest in her brother-in-law had to do with discussing the major's burial or establishing his guilt. Either way, the chaplain had made the offer, and Nate wouldn't withdraw it now. Besides, seeing the dynamic play out between the victim's sister and husband might reveal more information than Maggie had been willing to share.

Touching her elbow, Nate encouraged Maggie to stand. Corporal Mills approached, carrying her coat and handbag, which Nate took from him.

Nate handed Maggie her purse and helped her with her coat. "If you give me the keys, I'll have Mills drive your car to the BOQ and leave it there, while you and the chaplain and I talk to Mr. Hughes."

"What about Dani?" she asked as she placed the keys in Nate's outstretched hand.

"She'll be taken to the morgue. An autopsy will be performed sometime later today. Once you and Mr. Hughes determine how your sister should be buried, her body will be released to the funeral home. If you'd like, I can help you with the arrangements."

Nate was relieved to see her face soften. She attempted to smile. "Thank you."

Warmed by her response, he asked, "Is there anyone you'd like to call? A family member? Your mom? Maybe a boyfriend?"

Her eyes clouded as she shook her head. "My mother died a number of years ago. There's no one else."

Her loneliness in the midst of her grief cut him deeply. Upstairs the sound of footsteps indicated the body was being prepared for transport. It was time to get Maggie out of the house.

"My car's outside." Nate put his hand on the small of Maggie's back and urged her toward the door Corporal Mills held open. The chaplain grabbed her suitcase and followed them into the damp night air. Maggie wrapped her arms around her waist and accepted Nate's steadying hand on her elbow as she walked down the steps and settled into the front seat of his car, while the chaplain slid into the rear.

A light went on in the front bedroom of Lieutenant Colonel Foglio's quarters across the street. The curtain moved ever so slightly.

Looking back at Quarters 1448, Nate's eyes focused on the attic dormer window. The copycat suicide was unusual, and often little things made a difference in an investigation. The fact that Major Bennett had been barefoot when she died bothered him. But something else troubled Nate more.

The victim would have needed light to loop the rope over the crossbeam. Why would Major Bennett then turn off the light and take her own life in the dark?

TWO

Sitting next to Nate in the passenger seat, Maggie watched the headlights cut through the darkness, knowing she had kept information from the CID agent. She needed time to put some semblance of order to the confusion of her life before she made the decision to tell him.

Dani had implied some military law enforcement personnel couldn't be trusted. Maggie wasn't sure if that included the CID. Graham worked in the AmeriWorks contracting office and her sister hadn't mentioned the problem to him. Could the contractors be involved, as well?

It was hard to believe her sister was dead. Right when they were beginning to reconnect.

Oh, God, why? Maggie had been working on improving her relationship with the Lord. Hopefully He would provide the strength she needed.

Her parents, now Dani—

"Graham's staying at an apartment complex not far from post."

Nate's comment pulled her from a path to the past where memories cut like shards of glass. Tonight another tragedy left her riddled with grief and filled with questions.

From the backseat, the chaplain once again offered words of sympathy that Maggie appreciated but wasn't able to fully comprehend. The fact that Dani was dead seemed surreal. Maggie still refused to believe it could have been suicide.

Her sister had worked too hard to get where she was in the military to take her own life. Plus, if she had wanted to end it all, she wouldn't have chosen a noose.

The chaplain finished his discourse and settled back in his seat, giving Maggie an opportunity to glance at the agent sitting behind the wheel. Despite the civilian coat and tie he wore, Nate had military written all over him with his short haircut and intense gaze. He was probably a workaholic, who put the job first. Her father had fit that bill. Although so did she, if truth be told.

Just as Dani had turned to the military for fulfillment, Maggie had allowed counseling to take over her own life. They'd both learned from their dad, no doubt.

Riding across post in silence, Maggie concentrated on seeing Graham again. The last time they were together, Maggie had been in high school. Back then, he'd been the bad boy all the girls ran after. But people changed and maybe Graham had, as well.

Would she even recognize him after all these years? No matter what, she needed to be in control of her emotions and display strength instead of weakness. Dani deserved as much.

Nate drove through the main gate and turned onto a stretch of road lined with seedy bars, pawnshops and fast-food restaurants, all low-rent businesses that preyed on young soldiers far from home. Alabama had its fair share of ticky-tacky, but nothing compared with those hawking wares to the nation's youthful warriors.

"Shouldn't be much farther." Nate checked the address written on a sheet of paper. Eventually, he pulled into an apartment complex and braked to a stop in front of a row of two-story town houses.

"Wait in the car, Maggie. Once we've established Graham is in the house, I'll come back and get you."

Trying to appeal to his common sense, she opened the passenger door. "That will delay you. There's no reason why I can't go with you now."

"She's right." The chaplain stepped from the car and glanced at Nate.

"Whatever you say, sir."

Maggie heard a hint of frustration in Nate's reply. No telling how Graham would react to this dead-of-the-night encounter. The CID agent probably wondered if having her underfoot would complicate an already difficult situation. The look on his face sent a clear message he would rather leave her in the car.

Nate hadn't known her long enough to realize she could handle adversity. She'd had enough in her lifetime, although tonight wasn't the norm. She was acting on instinct rather than reason.

Falling into step between the two officers, Maggie was struck with the irony of the moment and the army's attention to detail. The powers that be had provided a chaplain to comfort the grieving husband and a CID agent to decide whether to haul him in for questioning. If Maggie had anything to say about what would unfold, she'd demand Graham be interrogated for hours until he divulged the truth about her sister's death.

Nate flicked his gaze around the apartment complex, making her realize that, if her brother-in-law was a killer, the three of them could be in danger. The hair on the back of her neck tingled as she took in the deep shadows and hidden recesses where someone—anyone—could be hiding.

Nate stepped protectively in front of her and knocked on the door. The three of them waited in silence.

"Yeah?" A deep voice sounded through the closed door.

"I'm Special Agent Patterson, of the U.S. Army CID, and I'm here with Chaplain Grant. We're looking for Graham Hughes."

The door opened, and a tall, beefy guy, wearing a T-shirt and flannel pajama bottoms, stood in the threshold. A scruffy beard and disheveled hair completed his attire.

Resting his hand on the doorjamb, he stared at them with confused eyes. "Something wrong?"

Nate pulled out his identification and held it open. "We need to speak to Graham Hughes."

"He's not here."

Glancing around Nate and into the apartment, Maggie saw a leather couch and a coffee table covered with newspapers and a pizza delivery box.

"Are you Arnold Zart?" Nate asked.

"Yeah." The guy stifled a yawn. "Who's the woman?"

"I'm Maggie Bennett," she said, in a voice that sounded more self-assured than she currently felt. "I'm Graham's sister-in-law."

"Any suggestions where we can find him?" Nate asked, deflecting the guy's attention away from Maggie.

"No clue."

"When was the last time you saw Mr. Hughes?" Nate continued.

"We work together. I saw him at the office yesterday, that would be Friday, and only briefly after work."

"Has he been living here with you?"

"Graham and his wife are having problems. I've got a spare bedroom and told him that he could bunk here until they patched things up."

"Did he mention reconciling with his wife?"

Zart dropped his arm. "Look, I'm not comfortable talking about Graham's personal life behind his back."

Nate squared his shoulders and leaned in closer. "I could take you to the CID office if you'd feel more comfortable there."

The guy held up his hands. "Give me a break, okay?" He hesitated and then sighed. "Graham said he was going over to the Freemont Bar and Grill on Johnson Street about nine o'clock last night. A woman works there. She's been interested in him for some time. Graham needed to talk."

"A woman?" Maggie blurted out unable to remain silent. "What's her name?"

The contractor shrugged. "Graham never said."

Nate gave him his card. "If Mr. Hughes comes back, have him call me."

"Will do." The guy shut the door, leaving them standing on the front steps.

"But—?" Maggie wanted more information.

Nate took her arm and turned her toward the street. "We'll talk in the car."

She pulled her arm from his hold and huffed as she

hurriedly walked along the sidewalk. "You could have searched the house."

"We don't have the authority—not at this point. But we'll track down the woman who works at the bar and grill. She might be able to lead us to Graham."

Maggie wrapped her arms around her waist, feeling tired as well as angry. "He's probably out of the country by now."

"More likely, he's with his new girlfriend."

"Well, that makes me feel better. He kills Dani and then finds another woman." She glared at Nate.

"His indiscretion may be reprehensible, but it doesn't prove he killed your sister."

"What does it prove?"

"That he's not the type of guy I'd want my sister to marry."

The sudden softness in his tone made her drop her defenses. Tears flooded her eyes. She missed her step and stumbled on the rough sidewalk.

Nate steadied her with his hand on her elbow. "It's late, Maggie. You need some sleep."

A lump settled in her throat and prevented her from speaking. Maybe the CID agent understood a bit more than she had realized. If only she could make him understand that her sister hadn't taken her own life. Maggie would do anything to convince him of the truth.

Once Maggie and the chaplain climbed into the car and buckled their seat belts, Nate pulled out of the apartment complex and onto the main road, leading back to Fort Rickman. He dug his cell phone out of his pocket, called Jamison and relayed what had happened.

"Have someone locate the owner of the bar and grill.

See if he knows Graham Hughes or the woman who has taken an interest in him. We might get lucky. Otherwise, we'll have to wait until he eventually returns to Zart's apartment. I'll see you when I get back to post."

Nate disconnected and flicked a glance over his shoulder to the chaplain. "Sorry to take up your time, sir."

"You think the husband was involved in Major Bennett's death?"

"He killed her," Maggie said with conviction. "Dani fought with him earlier and kicked him out. Easy enough for Graham to return later."

"We need evidence, Maggie, to prove a crime has been committed at all," Nate explained.

"Check his alibi with the woman he's supposed to be seeing. Threaten to involve her if she doesn't tell the truth." Nate almost smiled at Maggie's attempt to tell him how to handle the investigation.

"Search his car and the apartment where he's staying," she added. "You'll uncover something."

"And if we don't find any evidence that points to his guilt?"

"Then—"

The amateur sleuth seemed to have run out of options.

"Then throw him in jail until he talks," she finally said.

"You know we can't do that. But we will find him and determine where he was tonight."

"Focus on determining why he killed my sister." With another huff, Maggie turned toward the passenger window and stared into the night.

Nate glanced at the rearview mirror, catching the chaplain's eye. "At this point, sir, we don't know much. Hopefully the autopsy and toxicology results will shed more light on the situation."

"The 2nd Transportation Battalion has had a rough few days," the chaplain commented. "I'm sure you heard about the IED explosion that took two men in Afghanistan."

"Yes, sir. Were you involved in the notification?"

"The driver was unmarried. His parents live in New Jersey. An officer from Fort Dix visited them. But the company commander lived on post and left a wife and kids."

Nate heard struggle in Chaplain Grant's voice. Most days, Nate didn't think about God or the difficulty a man of faith might have in comforting the grieving. As a CID agent, his job was to ensure the family was notified, if a crime had been committed. He left the spiritual consolation to the chaplains. Still, he found himself searching for a way to reach out to Maggie, to ease the pain and frustration she was feeling and bring her comfort.

Nate glanced at Maggie again. If the tables were turned, he'd be lashing out, as well. Fact was, when his brother died, Nate had been filled with pain and anger. Some of which he still hadn't resolved.

"Might seem strange," the chaplain said from the rear, his voice melancholy. "But the commander's wife ended up comforting me. The woman has great faith in the Almighty. She's grieving, but she knows God didn't cause the IED explosion that took her husband's life."

Once upon a time, Nate had believed God protected

the faithful. Now, the memory of what had happened to Michael was never far from his mind. Truth be told, he blamed God as well as himself.

Glancing at Maggie, Nate said, "Seems impossible to trust a so-called loving God when your world falls apart."

She nodded slowly but kept her eyes trained on the passing darkness. Raindrops splattered against the windshield, adding to the oppressive gloom that had settled over all of them.

The chaplain sighed. "I don't have the answer, but I know we can't turn our backs on the Creator. He made us because He loves us, and His love is unconditional. I keep coming back to that. God knows all. How can I, as a finite creature, hope to understand why things happen? Maybe someday I'll see more clearly. Right now, I'm looking with human eyes that don't see the entire picture. I have to trust in Him. That's not always easy."

Trust in God wasn't high on Nate's priority list. Would he ever be able to soften his heart and turn to the Lord again?

What about Maggie? Would her sister's death have a long-term impact on her life, too? Maybe they'd talk about it sometime if he got to know her better.

Warmth spread through him again and his neck tingled. As much as Nate hated to admit it, even to himself, the woman's pain affected him deeply. Usually, he could trust his feelings. Tonight he wasn't sure of anything, especially when it involved Maggie Bennett.

She was alone and grieving. Nate thought of the other cases he had investigated. One death often led to another.

If he were a praying man, he'd ask that no one else—especially Maggie—would be hurt in any way by what had happened tonight.

THREE

Maggie scheduled an appointment to plan her sister's funeral with the chaplain for the following day before Nate dropped him off at his car. Once back on the main road, the CID agent turned warm eyes her way.

"Cold?" The light from the dash played over his lips that parted into an encouraging smile.

She shook her head. "I'm okay."

"The weatherman has predicted rain for another week. Hard to believe after the years of drought we've had in the Southeast. Now the rivers are threatening to overflow their banks, streams are swollen and..."

He was making small talk, probably to keep her mind off the tragedy. She looked back at the road, unable to think of anything *except* what had happened.

"I'm sorry about your sister," he finally offered.

"She didn't take her own life." Maggie might be driving home a point he didn't want to hear, but she had to convince this man with the genuine smile that suicide wasn't an option.

"Let me assure you, every effort will be made to learn the truth."

She sighed at the pat answer that didn't satisfy her.

"It's ironic that my sister survived a war zone only to be killed once she got home."

Glancing out the passenger window, Maggie stared into the darkness before asking, "Were you ever stationed in Afghanistan?"

"Twice."

"And you made it back okay?" She turned to face him.

His eyes narrowed, and he gazed at the road ahead as if seeing something more than pavement. A muscle in his neck twitched. "Yeah, but my brother didn't."

"I'm...I'm sorry." She picked at the sleeve of her sweater. "So then you understand?"

"What you're going through?" He nodded. "A death in the family is always hard, but especially so when it's unexpected."

He pulled in a lungful of air and glanced at her. "The shock makes everything hurt even more."

She saw his own struggle reflected back at her from crystal-blue eyes visible in the half light from the dash. The counselor in her wanted him to go deeper, but the set of his jaw told her that, as far as Nate was concerned, the subject was closed.

He pointed to a cluster of apartments that appeared in the distance. "Kelly lives in the first set of BOQs."

Maggie unbuckled her seat belt and grabbed her purse once he parked the car. Nate carried her suitcase and escorted her to the second apartment on the right where Kelly opened the door and motioned her inside.

"I know it's been a hard night," the female agent said to Maggie in greeting as she took the bag from Nate's hand.

Hot tears burned her eyes. Suddenly, she wanted

to get away from Nate Patterson and his sympathetic friend. To his credit, he didn't come in, but said goodbye at the door.

Kelly led the way to the guest room where a pink gingham comforter, trimmed with eyelet, covered a twin bed with a white wicker headboard. A matching nightstand and rocker sat nearby. Kelly placed Maggie's suitcase on a blanket chest at the foot of the bed.

"You'll find towels in the bathroom just across the hall. May I get you a cup of tea? Maybe something to eat?"

"I just need some sleep."

"Of course you do. If you get up before I do, the coffeepot will be ready to turn on. There's cream in the fridge. Sugar's on the counter. Help yourself to cereal or eggs, whatever you want for breakfast."

"Thank you, Kelly."

"Not a problem. See you in the morning."

Once the other woman left the bedroom and closed the door behind her, Maggie collapsed onto the bed and put her head in her hands. Tears streamed down her cheeks.

She tried to bring stability and peace to the families she counseled, but right now, she needed help herself. The harsh reality was she felt totally alone.

Maggie woke with a start, hearing the phone ring in the living room of Kelly's quarters. Visions of Dani had circled through her dreams for the few hours she'd been asleep and now returned to haunt her when her eyes were wide open.

Still wearing her jeans and orange sweater, Maggie pulled herself from the bed and glanced at the items she had packed in her suitcase. Something seemed out of place, giving her an uneasy feeling. She shrugged it off, realizing that it was probably because she had been in such a hurry last night.

She grabbed a fresh outfit and stepped into the bathroom across the hall to change, surprised by the woman staring back at her from the mirror. She hadn't expected to see dark circles under her eyes.

Death takes a heavy toll on those left behind. Her mother's words flowed from the past.

Returning to the hallway, Maggie followed the smell of coffee to the kitchen where Kelly stood at the counter, holding half of a bagel slathered with cream cheese and jelly. "Morning. Did the phone wake you?"

"No, I was up." Not quite the truth, but Maggie didn't want to discuss her restless night.

Kelly pointed to a clean mug, sitting next to the coffeepot. "Help yourself."

"Thanks." Maggie poured a cup and drank it black.

"The phone call was from Chief Agent-in-Charge Wilson. He's the head of our CID unit at Rickman. There's a problem involving a soldier in North Georgia that I have to check into, which might take a couple of days. The guy was part of the 2nd Transportation Battalion."

"My sister's unit."

Kelly nodded. "This guy came home early because he needed surgery and had been on convalescent leave ever since."

She didn't provide any additional information. Probably more bad news. "I'll get my things if you can suggest a motel in town," Maggie said.

"Nonsense. No reason you can't stay here while I'm

gone. Nate lives in an apartment across the open stair-well if you need anything."

Maggie thought of the warmth of his gaze in the car last night. "Are you sure you don't mind?"

"I insist. Speaking of Nate, he's been working all night, but he's headed over here now. He wants to talk to you."

Hopefully, he had located Graham.

"Help yourself to anything in the refrigerator." Opening a cabinet drawer, Kelly pulled out a small phone directory. "We've got delivery pizza and Chinese carry-out on post. The numbers are highlighted in the book. Better yet, have Nate grill a couple steaks. Tell him Kelly said to make his special garlic mashed potatoes and Caesar salad."

"I'm sure I won't go hungry." Maggie was surprised to learn Nate cooked. Her father had never lifted his hand in the kitchen. For some reason, she'd thought all military guys would be the same.

A car door slammed outside. "Bet that's him now." Kelly crammed the last bite of bagel into her mouth. Chewing, she washed her hands and looked out the window before she headed for the door.

"How about some breakfast?" Kelly motioned Nate inside.

"Thanks, but I'll take a rain check."

Maggie raked her fingers though her hair and fluffed the bangs off her forehead. Not that she cared about the way she looked, but last night Nate had been—

"Morning, Maggie." He stepped into the kitchen, bringing a hint of the wet outdoors with him. Despite his all-night work marathon, he was clean-shaven and alert. Even his white shirt had maintained its starch.

"Coffee?" Kelly opened a cabinet and reached for a mug.

"I don't have time." He pulled a black-and-white photo printout from a folder and dropped it onto the table. "Maggie, one of our men pulled this off your sister's laptop. Does it mean anything to you?"

She stared at the picture of a potbellied earthenware figurine.

"The original is housed in the Kabul Museum," Nate continued. "Probably from the third or fourth century when the silk routes wove through what is Afghanistan today." He glanced down at the photo, then back at her. "Growing up, did your sister have an interest in ancient artifacts?"

"Not that I recall. Maybe she visited the museum while she was in Afghanistan?"

He shook his head. "It's doubtful. Her unit wasn't in that area. She downloaded the photos the day before she redeployed home. When you met with her, did she mention anything about researching artifacts?"

Not artifacts, necessarily, but over lunch, Dani *had* mentioned mailing an item stateside that would provide evidence she could take to the provost marshal on post, though she hadn't shared only details with Maggie.

Nate was staring at her. "Did you think of something?"

"No." She shook her head a little too quickly. The way he continued to stare, she wondered if he could read her mind.

Finally, she said, "Dani liked to immerse herself in the culture of the countries she visited. My hunch would be she had heard about the figurine and wanted to learn more."

Kelly glanced at the photo still lying on the table. "Sure is a strange-looking little man."

"Did you find anything else on her computer?" Maggie asked.

"Not on her hard drive." Nate pulled another paper from the folder. "But your sister had a list of names and addresses tucked inside a book on her nightstand." He looked at Maggie. "Do any of these people sound familiar?"

Nate read from the list. "Reginald Samuel. Lance Davis. Kendra Adams."

"Kendra Adams?"

"You know her?"

"I…" Maggie hesitated. "A girl by that name attended Freemont High School when we lived here. She and Dani were friends."

"Did your sister keep in touch with her after you left Fort Rickman?"

"Not that I'm aware of, but I told you, Dani and I hadn't seen each other in a number of years."

Nate appeared to accept her answer, then read the remainder of the list aloud before he raised his brow. "Do you recognize anyone else?"

Maggie shook her head. "Only Kendra. What address do you have for her?"

"A post office box in Mansell, Georgia, about fifteen miles east of here."

"She used to live in downtown Freemont," Maggie said. "What are the other addresses?"

Nate held the paper out so she could read the listings. "They're all post office boxes in neighboring towns."

Kelly arched her brows. "Strange, huh?"

Nate tried to brush it off with a shrug, but Maggie

knew the names and addresses were important or he wouldn't have mentioned them. "Has anything else come to light?"

He shook his head. "The autopsy won't be done until this afternoon. We might have more answers then."

"Did you talk to Graham?"

Nate hesitated for a long moment. "We haven't been able to locate him."

Maggie let out a sigh of frustration. "As I mentioned last night, he probably hightailed it to Atlanta and booked a flight out of the country. Aren't the first forty-eight hours the most critical in a murder investigation?"

"Is it a murder case?" Kelly glanced from Maggie to Nate.

"As I said, we'll have more information after the autopsy." Nate's voice was firm. "There were no signs of struggle. The door was locked when you entered the house."

"Graham could have easily locked the door behind him. And what about the footsteps I heard?"

"The wind was strong last night. Old houses settle. The creaks can be deceptive."

Thinking back, she wasn't sure what she had heard. Maybe Nate was right about the footsteps, but he was wrong if he still thought Dani's death was suicide. He needed to find Graham and haul him in for questioning.

"Did you know your sister was taking antianxiety medication?" Nate asked.

The question caught her off guard. "Are you sure?"

"We found a half-empty bottle of Xanax in her kitchen cabinet prescribed by an off-post physician and filled at a civilian pharmacy."

"Which doesn't prove she killed herself."

"I never said it did."

Anger bubbled up within her. "But that was the direction you were headed, wasn't it? *Mentally unbalanced major takes her own life.* I can see the headlines in the local paper."

Before Nate could respond, his cell rang. He pulled it to his ear, checking caller ID en route. "Hey, Jamison."

Nate looked down at the table. "Roger that. I'll head there now."

Returning the phone to his pocket, he turned to Kelly. "I've got to go to headquarters."

"Something turn up?"

"They located Graham."

Nate shoved the papers back into his folder then glanced at Maggie. "I'll talk to your brother-in-law about the arrangements for internment and drive you to the funeral home this afternoon, say about 1300 hours. One o'clock."

The CID agent with the deep-set eyes was building a case against Dani. Maggie's first impression of Nate had been good, and in a strange way, she felt attracted to him, but if he believed her sister had taken her own life then—

A door slammed as Nate left.

Maggie walked to the window and watched him drive away. A mixture of sadness and resolve rolled over her. If Nate believed Dani had taken her own life, Maggie would do just about anything to prove him wrong.

Even confront Graham.

Initially, she had thought he had killed her sister because of the divorce, but if Graham was involved in the illegal activity Dani had uncovered, he would have had even more motive to take her life.

Another thought came to mind that sent a chill down Maggie's spine. If Graham hadn't killed her, some other conspirator could have realized Dani was getting too close and decided she needed to be silenced. The person who killed her sister had struck once. What would stop him from killing again?

FOUR

Nate's first impression of Graham Hughes wasn't good. He smelled like day-old sweat and stale beer, and from the looks of his bloodshot eyes, he had evidently tied one on last night.

The husband of the deceased stood at least six-two and appeared to know his way around a weight room. All that muscle could easily overpower a woman, yet any use of force would leave telltale marks on the victim.

While Major Bennett's exposed limbs had been free of bruises, the autopsy might reveal something hidden by her clothing. Nate would know soon enough.

"You went to the bar at 2300 hours?"

"Eleven o'clock? That's right." Graham nodded to Nate from across the table. "Wanda and I were together from then on. The bartender can tell you. We stayed at the bar and grill until it closed at 2:00 a.m. Then we went back to her apartment. I was still there when Mr. Steele knocked on her door this morning."

Wanda had confirmed Graham's alibi, which had been corroborated by the apartment security guard. He said Graham's red Mustang convertible had remained parked next to Wanda's Highlander from 2:00 a.m. on. Unless Graham had snuck out of the bar, gone to post and gotten back before heading to Wanda's apartment, his alibi seemed tight.

Nate threw out a number of questions in rapid succession, but Graham's answers never varied from the initial responses he had given Jamison. Eventually, Nate mentioned burial arrangements.

"Whatever Maggie wants is fine with me."

One less problem for Maggie to worry about, for which Nate was grateful.

"How is she?" Graham asked. His eyes were soulful as he stared at Nate. "Maggie's a good person. She doesn't need more pain in her life."

"No one does, Mr. Hughes."

"You got that right."

Graham glanced down at his clasped hands resting on the tabletop and shook his head. "I should have known it wouldn't work out for Dani and me."

"How's that?"

"It might sound strange, but I sometimes wondered if Dani married me just to qualify for quarters on post. She lived in the Hunter Housing Area as a kid. The nice brick homes are usually reserved for lieutenant colonels, but a number of units were vacant when we started dating and it was common knowledge the post housing office planned to open the quarters to married majors just to get the vacancies filled."

"So she got the house. What did you gain from the marriage?"

"Validation. I've made a lot of mistakes. Dani made me feel like I'd finally turned my life around."

Nate understood about making mistakes, but what mistakes did Graham have in his past? Had they caused his marriage to fall apart—or was that the result of other mistakes, ones he was making now? "When did you and Wanda start seeing each other?"

"I kept my distance until last night after my wife made it clear our marriage was over."

Nate scooted his chair away from the table. "I'm sorry for your loss, Mr. Hughes. Don't leave the area in case we need to get in touch with you."

He met up with Jamison in the hallway. The fashionably dressed agent held up a manila folder. "I've got an address for Kendra Adams. A street of older row houses located in an area of town known for crime."

"Let's go."

"No can do. The boss wants an update. I contacted the local authorities and filled them in."

"That's a help. Thanks." Nate glanced at his watch. He had told Maggie he would drive her to the funeral home at 1300. One o'clock. That gave him more than an hour to talk to Kendra.

As he drove across town, Nate tried to keep his mind on the case instead of the struggle he'd seen play over Maggie's pretty face and troubled eyes this morning. Last night, she'd pointed a finger at Graham, yet the man's alibi was tight as an ammo canister. No matter how fetching Maggie seemed, she was undeniably fragile, as well. Was the stress of the situation making her irrational? It seemed so obvious that the major had committed suicide. Why did Maggie refuse to see it?

Approaching the street Jamison had mentioned, Nate signaled before he turned left. Halfway down the block, he spied a woman with mocha skin, wearing a colorful caftan and a matching scarf around her head. She stepped away from a second woman whose back was to the street. The wind teased auburn hair around the second woman's slender shoulders as she waved her hands in the air.

Maggie?

Nate pulled to the curb and threw open the door. Slamming it closed behind him, he double-timed across the street.

The woman in the caftan raised her voice. "Get outta here. Leave me alone." She turned on her heel.

Maggie caught her arm. "You can't walk away from this, Kendra."

The anger written across the face of the woman Maggie had called Kendra was evident even to Nate. He had to do something before the discussion got out of hand.

"Maggie," he called.

She let go of Kendra's arm and turned. "What are you doing here, Nate?"

"I could ask you the same thing."

Maggie glanced back at the other woman. "I was talking to Kendra Adams."

The woman put her hands on her hips and stared at Nate. "Who are you?"

He held out his identification. "U.S. Army CID. I need to talk to you, Ms. Adams." Nate glanced at the row of homes on the street. "Might be a good idea to move our conversation inside."

Narrowing her eyes, Kendra looked over her shoulder. An elderly woman pulled back an upstairs curtain in the next-door dwelling and stared down at where Nate and the two women stood on the cracked sidewalk.

Expelling a deep sigh, Kendra turned and stomped up her steps. "You two had best come inside then."

The house was modestly furnished, but clean and neat. Kendra pointed Nate and Maggie toward a flowered couch and sat across from them on an overstuffed chair decorated in the same floral print.

"Like I told you outside, I don't know anything about Dani anymore." Kendra looked first at Maggie and then switched her gaze to Nate. "If she's in trouble, it has nothing to do with me."

"Your name along with an address for a post office box in Manning, Georgia, were uncovered in her quarters," Nate said. "Do you have any idea why?"

"Maybe she planned to write to me." Kendra's voice was spiked with attitude.

"For what reason?"

The woman pointed a finger back at her own chest. "Like I should know? Ask Dani."

Nate ignored Kendra's sarcastic reply. "Have you and Major Bennett kept in touch since high school?"

"She moved away in our junior year. That was the last I saw her."

"What about when she came back to post?"

She shrugged. "I ran into Dani downtown once about two years ago. We said hello, talked for a few minutes. That was it."

"You're sure that's the only time you've talked?" he pressed.

Kendra lifted her brow. "I'm very sure. You can ask Dani."

"Unfortunately, I can't. Major Bennett died last night."

Kendra's eyes widened. "She's dead?"

Maggie nodded. "Murdered."

Nate didn't confirm or deny the comment. He'd let the mention of murder add to the anxiety pulling at Kendra's face. He still believed the major's death was suicide, but if she and Kendra had gotten mixed up in something dangerous—maybe something involving shipments into the U.S.—it might explain why she'd taken her own life.

Kendra rolled her eyes upward, and then covered her cheeks with her hands and moaned. "Oh, my God in heaven."

Nate softened his tone. "Tell us what you and Dani were doing with that Manning P.O. box."

Kendra dropped her hands and straightened her shoulders. Fear flashed in her eyes, but her jaw steeled with determination. "I don't know anything about a P.O. box."

At that moment, a rustle sounded from the hallway. Glancing over his shoulder, Nate saw a small child, probably four or five years old, peering into the living room.

"Mama?"

"Baby cakes, you scoot on into the kitchen. Mama left a sandwich for you on the table. Be a good girl now and eat your lunch."

Wide-eyed, the child raced through a swinging door at the end of the dining area and disappeared from sight.

Nate turned his focus back to Kendra. "Let me repeat my earlier question. What do you know about a post office box in Manning, Georgia?"

"Absolutely nothing." She stared back at him for a long moment and then dropped her gaze.

Reaching into his pocket, Nate pulled out his cell phone. "I'm sworn to defend and protect the Constitution, ma'am. Part of my responsibilities involves protecting children who might be in danger. Excuse me while I contact Child Services. They'll want to talk to you about any illegal activities with which you might be associated."

He tapped in a series of digits, his eyes on the phone. From the tension in the room, Nate knew Kendra was weighing her options. If she were the dutiful mother she appeared to be, he expected the woman's memory to improve within the next few seconds.

As he entered the seventh digit and placed the phone to his ear, Kendra held up her hand. "Wait."

He glanced up.

"I'll tell you what I know." She sighed and slumped back in the chair.

He hit the disconnect button and lowered the phone. "I'm listening."

"A man contacted me one night. I was in a bad way, struggling to make ends meet." She shrugged. "He said I could earn a little extra. Buy some nice things for my child. So I asked the man what I had to do. He told me to rent a box at the post office in Manning. He said his friend would call me when a special package arrived addressed to me."

"Did he tell you what the package would contain?"

"No. And I didn't ask. About three weeks later, I got a phone call, telling me a box had arrived."

"What else?"

"That's all he said. I drove to Manning and picked up the package. The caller said I was to deliver it to Wally's Pawn."

"On Military Drive?" Nate asked.

"That's it. A man by the name of LeShawn took the package and paid me for my trouble."

"Did he open the box while you were there?"

"No. He put it in a back room. Then he gave me seventy-five dollars and told me someone would call if they needed me again."

"How many packages have you received?"

"Hmm?" She looked at the ceiling. "At least five. No, six boxes in the last year."

"Do you remember the return address or the name of the sender?"

"They were all different names from different military APOs. I can't remember anything specific."

"Who contacted you, Kendra?"

"He never told me his name."

"And you have no idea what the boxes contained?"

She shook her head.

Maggie scooted forward on the couch. "What if they're smuggling something illegal into the United States? If Dani was looking into it then maybe she was killed because of what she had learned."

A low, guttural sound crept up from deep within Kendra. She glanced furtively toward the kitchen. The look on her face revealed the gravity of the mistake she had made.

"I never would have gotten involved, except my daughter has medical problems, which means specialists and medication. Money's always tight."

"Did you recognize the voice of the men who called you?" Maggie asked.

Kendra shook her head.

"Could one of them have been Graham?"

"Graham Hughes?" She thought for a moment. "I'm not sure. Maybe. I heard he and Dani were together again." Kendra's eyes widened. "You think he's involved?"

"We're not sure of anything at this point," Nate said. "But should this turn into a criminal investigation, Ms. Adams, the authorities will look more leniently on you if you continue to provide information." He gave her his card. "I don't have to tell you, you may be in danger. Feel free to call me at any time."

Maggie dug in her purse and pulled out her own business card. She hastily wrote down Kelly's landline phone number, too. Handing it to Kendra, she said, "Call me if you need to talk. My cell is listed on the front of the card. The number of where I'm staying is on the back."

Leaving the house, Nate sensed Maggie's concern about Kendra's safety. "I'll alert the local police to increase surveillance in this area. The FBI and Postal Inspectors need to be brought onboard, as well."

"Do you think it is a smuggling operation?"

"More than likely, based on her description. It's a classic setup. When we get to the other people on your sister's list, I'm sure we'll hear a lot of similar stories."

Maggie glanced back at Kendra's house. "She must have been desperate."

"Which is when people often make mistakes. I want you to drive back to post while I stop at the pawnshop. I'll let you know if I learn anything new."

Maggie shook her head. "If this involves Dani, I'm going with you. Besides…" She gave him a quick once-over. "Dressed in that coat and tie, you hardly look like the typical pawnshop clientele."

"You don't fit the bill, either, Ms. Bennett."

"No, but together we might be able to pull it off. We'll say I'm interested in pawned jewelry."

"What am I, your jewelry consultant? I don't like it, Maggie."

"Do you have another option?"

"I'll change clothes and come back undercover."

"Which will waste time."

"Go back to post, Maggie. I want to keep you safe."

Her brow raised. "Then you can play the role of my protective boyfriend." She turned and headed to her silver Saturn, leaving him to stare after her.

Protective boyfriend?

As Maggie slipped behind the wheel, Nate opened the door to his own car and then turned to look over his shoulder. A dark-colored sedan sat parked at the end of the block. Although the windows were tinted, someone appeared to be hunkered down behind the wheel.

The person could have pulled off the road to talk on his cell phone or he could be waiting for someone. Neither option seemed to fit. Was the driver there because of them, because of the talk they'd had with Kendra?

Nate's gut tightened as he thought of Kendra's adorable daughter, knowing what could happen because her mother had gotten involved with people working outside the law.

Then he thought of Major Bennett's body hanging from a noose. If she had been involved with a smuggling operation and didn't know how to untangle herself, suicide could have provided a way out. But if she hadn't been involved and instead had stumbled onto something illegal, that knowledge may have led to her murder.

Nate glanced at Maggie, who was adjusting the rearview mirror in her car. In jest, she had mentioned a protective boyfriend. If her sister had been murdered, Maggie would need more than a boyfriend to protect her. She would need a special agent to keep her alive.

FIVE

Maggie turned her Saturn into the pawnshop parking lot and braked to a stop next to Nate just before a sedan drove past. She had spied the car in her rearview mirror shortly after leaving Kendra's neighborhood. Now, seeing the vehicle zip out of sight, her uneasiness grew. Why would anyone have tailed her to the pawnshop?

"Follow my lead," Nate said, as she stepped onto the pavement. "Don't give anything away. And don't mention Kendra or the list of names."

Did the man think she had no sense? She let out an exasperated sigh. "I may not be involved with law enforcement, but I do know how to keep a secret."

He raised his brow.

"What?" she asked, nonplussed by his expression.

He continued to stare at her, causing a nervous tingle along the side of her neck.

"I'm not saying that I have any secrets, if that's the reason for that silly expression on your face. Besides, we were talking about *not* tipping our hands to the pawnshop owner. You're becoming paranoid. Probably too much focus on your job. Aren't all military guys overachievers?"

His lips formed a smile. "That's debatable. Besides, you're the one who keeps mentioning secrets. I'm trying to learn what's being mailed to the people on the list we found in your sister's quarters."

"Then we're working toward the same goal."

His smile faded. "Are we, Maggie?"

"Why the verbal cat-and-mouse game, Nate? Do you think I'm not interested in the truth?"

"I'm just wondering what's making you uptight."

Her mouth dropped open. "Uptight?"

Maggie straightened her shoulders and tried to still the sporadic pounding of her heart, which—no matter what he thought—was not brought on by any lack of truthfulness on her part.

Rather, that dizzying feeling came from the way his eyes seemed to see beneath her skin to the very essence of who she really was, as if Nate had the ability to strip away the layers she wrapped protectively around her heart. She'd always been the shy wallflower next to her outgoing sister. It was disconcerting to have someone look that closely at her.

Needing to set him straight without delay, she widened her eyes and pursed her lips for emphasis. "The last thing I am is uptight or nervous."

Nate reached for a strand of hair that had blown across her cheek. His finger skimmed her flesh, causing a streak of lightning to zip along her spine. Gooseflesh rose on her arms, which she rubbed, hoping to halt her body's unexpected reaction to his touch.

In an attempt to cover her own confusion, Maggie returned the look Nate had given her with a levelheaded stare punctuated with a firm set of her jaw and narrowed eyes. "Let's get this done. Remember you're helping me find jewelry."

"And we're dating, right?"

Another jolt to her midsection. She needed to get her emotions under control lest Nate read more into the relationship than two people working to uncover the truth.

Truth? There it was again.

"Do you have any idea what the packages Kendra intercepted could contain?" Maggie needed to redirect the conversation.

"Drugs would be my guess. Afghanistan produces more than ninety percent of the world's heroin supply. A kilo of the pure stuff in country—in Afghanistan—runs about $5,000. By the time it hits the streets in the U.S., it can bring in up to $300,000. That's a profit some men can't resist."

"So we're looking for white powder?"

"The purer the heroin, the whiter the color. It can also be dirty brown, though. There's a black heroine that comes in from Mexico known as black tar. But we need to be on the lookout for *anything* that could be shipped from the Middle East to the U.S. illegally."

"Such as?" she pressed.

"Precious gems, even artifacts."

Like the earthenware figurine pictured in the computer photo pulled from her sister's laptop. Dani may have had problems when she was young, but no matter what Nate might think, her sister would never have gotten involved with an illegal operation. Maggie wasn't as sure about Graham.

She rolled her eyes. "So we're looking for precious

stones, ancient artifacts, powder in an assortment of colors or all of the above?"

"Basically, yes."

"Humph." She put her hands on her hips and paused for effect. "That certainly narrows down our search."

Without waiting for a response, she walked toward the pawnshop. As attractive as Nate might be, his efficient cop demeanor could be annoying at times. Especially his recent insinuations that she was holding something back, something he seemed to feel would point to Dani's culpability in a smuggling ring. As far as Maggie was concerned, she had a right to keep certain information under wraps. She owed that to her sister's memory. She also owed it to herself.

Pushing on the glass door, she stepped into the dimly lit interior. Nate followed her inside. Both of them stood, taking in the eclectic assortment of items people pawned for money—everything from electric knife sharpeners and mixing bowls to camcorders and cameras. Rows of shelves were jammed with computers, DVD recorders and other electronic items.

The merchandise seemed positioned to catch the eye of the soldiers, who frequented the pawnshops. If they were anything like the down-on-their-luck folks in Alabama, the troops stopped in close to payday when their bank accounts were empty and their families needed to be fed.

Not that she was passing judgment. She glanced at Nate who was doing a one-eighty, probably making a mental log of everything he saw.

According to what Maggie could determine, he was a take-charge guy who never saw a problem he couldn't fix. But was there something more below the surface?

Something he kept hidden from the world? He'd tensed when mentioning his brother's death. Undoubtedly, Mr. Special Agent had his own cross to carry.

A noise caused her to turn as a young man, mid-twenties, sporting facial hair and glasses, stepped through a fading, burnt sienna curtain that separated the front of the store from a room in the rear. Maggie tried to catch sight of what lay behind the divider but all she could see was a pile of corrugated boxes and more clutter.

The rumpled T-shirt and baggy jeans the clerk wore seemed in keeping with the lack of cleanliness everywhere Maggie looked. Focusing her attention back on him, she realized the pawned items would require time for her and Nate to examine them and perhaps provide an opportunity for the clerk to reveal something he shouldn't, such as a bit of information that might have bearing on her sister's death.

Digging deep within, Maggie pulled out a sunny disposition to go along with the smile she didn't feel but plastered across her lips. She forced a buoyancy into her step as she picked her way toward the clerk who had taken up residence behind one of the display cases.

"I'm interested in jewelry," Maggie said. "Pearls, silver, gold, precious stones."

The kid's expression lightened up a bit. "Don't see much gold these days. Most folks sell it for cash. The jeweler down the street gets most of that business." He pointed to the north, never realizing he might be encouraging an interested shopper to go elsewhere.

"Are you the owner?" Maggie asked, trying to pump up the guy's ego, even though there was no way Mr.

Goatee with the pudgy, baby cheeks could manage a business, even one in such disarray as Wally's Pawn.

The kid shook his head. "Wally owns the place. I work part-time."

"And you are…?"

"Ronald Jones. Most folks call me Bubba."

"Nice to meet you, Bubba." She glanced around the store. "Can you point out some of your better jewelry items for sale?"

"There are a few silver bracelets in the showcase by the window." Maggie followed his gaze and spied an assortment of thin bangles and silver-plated charm bracelets.

"Anything foreign?" She tried to hold Bubba's attention as Nate meandered around the store, feigning boredom. More than likely, he was casing the place, searching for anything that seemed suspicious.

"There's a set of stacking dolls from Russia." Bubba pointed over his shoulder to the top shelf. "They're hand painted. 'Course, one's broken."

"Could I see them?"

"Yes, ma'am." As he turned to retrieve the children's toy, Maggie shot Nate a questioning glance.

He shrugged. Evidently unable to find anything that looked significant, he nodded toward the orange curtain.

"Here you are." Bubba placed the stacking dolls on the glass-topped counter, looking proud of his offering.

Glancing at the now-empty spot on the shelf where the dolls had once been, Maggie spied a ceramic statue of a rather stout figure, which could have been a distant cousin to the one in the photo pulled from Dani's computer.

At least that's what Maggie thought until Bubba placed the figurine in her outstretched hand. Instead of a piece of antiquity, she saw a hand-glazed Friar Tuck of Robin Hood fame.

Maggie motioned to Nate. "Come here, and see the cutest little dolls Bubba found for me. Plus there's an unusual statue you might like."

Stepping to her side, Nate almost laughed at the comical friar, then fighting back his mirth, he turned to gaze playfully into her eyes. "But I thought you were interested in jewelry, my love."

His exaggeration should have caused her to at least smile. Instead, she felt overpowered by his nearness and tried in vain to quiet her rapid pulse and pounding heart. Their boyfriend-girlfriend charade was proving dangerous to her health. Undoubtedly, she had underestimated Nate's ability to get into character.

"You folks from around here?" Bubba asked.

"Alabama." Noting the clerk's confused frown, Maggie wrapped her arm around Nate's elbow and snuggled close. "My honey's stationed at Fort Rickman. I drove over this afternoon."

Bubba's frown turned upward. "We get lots of military folks in here."

"I bet you do." Maggie stood poised to pull back her arm as soon as the clerk turned away. However, Bubba continued to stare at them with a smug look on his face that could mean anything.

Nate disentangled himself from her grasp and then proceeded to drape his arm around her shoulder and lower his cheek to smell her hair. An explosive warning went off in her brain that ricocheted through her body.

Too close for comfort, the warning kept playing through her head.

"Now, sweetie." Nate's voice was mellow like chocolate. "I told you I'd buy you something pretty today."

"Promise?"

"Cross my heart." Nate shifted his gaze from her to the curtain. "Do you have anything in the back, Bubba? Maybe a big-ticket item?"

The clerk pursed his lips but didn't move.

Nate rubbed his fingers along Maggie's arm, causing an assortment of erratic sensations to tangle through her anatomy.

"Something wrong, sweetie? You seem a bit standoffish." Nate's eyes twinkled, causing her heart rate to increase even more. If she wasn't careful, she'd be in danger of cardiac arrest. She pulled in a steadying breath determined he wouldn't get the best of her. Besides, two could play this game.

Maggie wrapped both arms around Nate's neck and batted her lashes, pleased to see a pulse spot pound on his forehead. Keeping her eyes on the special agent, she said, "Bubba, you wanna check in the back room in case you've got any jewelry I might be interested in buying?"

The kid hopped from one foot to the other, then flicked his gaze to the orange curtain, looking ill at ease by their obvious display of affection. Or was there something in the rear room he didn't want to reveal?

His cheeks reddened. "I'll be back in a flash."

Bubba hustled through the curtain, leaving Maggie with her arms wrapped around Nate and her heart doing somersaults. His breath came in shallow pulls. A purely masculine lime scent teased her nose. Her neck warmed, and she no longer thought of Bubba or the back room. Instead she was totally focused on the tiny scar on Nate's chin, his parted lips and the lazy way his eyes were taking her in as if he were a giant magnet, drawing her close.

Time stopped and all she knew was the strength of Nate's embrace and a sense of security that wrapped around her like a warm blanket on a cold night.

"I found something you might like." Bubba stepped through the curtain.

The sound of his voice brought Maggie back to reality. No matter how good Nate felt, she didn't belong in his arms. She stepped away, but her skin continued to tingle where their flesh had touched. For an instant, her equilibrium faltered.

Nate grabbed her arm. "You okay, honey?"

The sincerity of his voice caused another bubble of warmth to boil within her. Pulling in a short breath, she smiled, slipping back into character. "I'm fine, sweetie. Let's see what Bubba found."

The clerk placed a small cigar box on the counter and opened the lid with a flourish. "Look at this," he said unable to mask the enthusiasm in his voice. The box contained a rhinestone brooch, probably circa 1940s, with matching screw-back earrings.

"They're very nice, Bubba, but not exactly what I'm looking for." She glanced at Nate. "What do you think?"

"Honey, whatever you like is fine with me."

Maggie checked her watch. "It's almost noon. Why don't we think about it over lunch?"

Bubba's face dropped somewhat. "You sure you folks don't want to buy the pin and earrings now?"

Nate pointed to the showcase by the wall. "I'd like to take a closer look at the .45 caliber you've got for sale."

"While you guys talk guns, I need to freshen up before we go to the restaurant," Maggie said. "Bubba, could you point me to your restroom?"

"In the back."

"Through the curtain?"

"That's right. On the left."

Nate's eyes held a glint of appreciation for what she'd accomplished.

As the men headed for the distant display case, Maggie slid between the panels of the curtain. The back room was small and even more cluttered than the main showroom.

Knowing she had to make every minute count, she looked in the stack of boxes and did a quick inventory of the piles of items on the floor. A desk sat in the corner. Holding her breath, she slid open the drawers and rifled through a number of manila files, none of which provided any information that seemed pertinent to the boxes being shipped into the U.S.

Stepping into the restroom, Maggie ran the water in the sink to cover any noise she might make as she opened an assortment of cardboard cartons piled on the concrete floor. Most were empty. A few contained garden tools and other yard equipment, but she found nothing of value nor anything that might be smuggled illegally into the United States.

The bell on the outside door tingled. "How's it going, Bubba?" A deep voice filtered through the curtain.

"Hey, LeShawn. You workin' this afternoon?"

"Wally wants me to do inventory." The voice and accompanying footsteps drew closer.

Her heart thumped a warning. A man named Le-Shawn had paid Kendra for delivering the mailed package.

Maggie closed the carton she was examining and then realized she had left the water running in the restroom. Racing for the sink, she placed her hand on the faucet just as a tall guy, probably six-three, pulled back the drape.

"Morning." She smiled, ignoring the startled look on his long face. Too late, she spied the desk drawer she'd inadvertently left open. There was nothing she could do at this point except exit stage right.

Halfway to the curtain, LeShawn grabbed her arm. "What's going on, lady?"

Despite her runaway pulse, Maggie narrowed her eyes and glared up at him. Her voice was low when she spoke. "You probably noticed my boyfriend out front. He's packing heat and doesn't like anything to upset me."

LeShawn stared at her for a long moment while her mouth dried to cotton and her heart hammered in her ear.

Finally, he released his hold.

A wave of relief washed over Maggie. She turned on her heel, stepped through the curtain and slipped back into girlfriend mode.

Motioning to Nate, Maggie trained her eyes on the young clerk. "Thanks, Bubba, for letting me use your restroom. We'll be back later if we decide to buy the rhinestone pin."

She started for the door, arm-in-arm with Nate, but

stopped short when a thought hit. Turning, she smiled once again at Bubba and then at LeShawn, who had pulled back the curtain and was staring at her.

"Have you seen any small earthenware potbellied figurines in your shop, Bubba?" she asked.

Nate glanced at the clerk, while his fingers tightened on Maggie's arm.

Bubba failed to hide the surprise that washed over his baby face. His neck flushed and he tried to speak. "Ah…ah…"

"That's not something we ever see around here, lady." LeShawn quickly helped him out.

Bubba's hesitation and LeShawn's attempt to fill in the blanks were telling. At least one of them, if not both, *had* seen earthenware potbellied figurines.

Maggie had learned something significant, but there was another question she needed to have answered. What role did the ancient artifact play in her sister's death?

SIX

Driving back to post from the pawnshop, Nate glanced in his rearview mirror at Maggie, who was following him in her own car. Using his side mirrors, he searched for the dark sedan he'd seen earlier. The car had trailed him and Maggie all the way from Kendra's house to Wally's Pawn. Nate had alerted the police, who promised to increase surveillance in that neighborhood, but he continued to be concerned about Maggie's safety.

She had done an amazing job with Bubba at the pawnshop. The woman had the instincts of a cop. Nate almost chuckled. Then he thought of the way she'd felt in his arms. When she'd snuggled close, his world had gone into aftershock. Talk about vertigo. Everything had swirled around him, except Maggie. He hadn't been able to take his eyes off her.

Pulling into the BOQ area, he waited as she parked and climbed into his car. A light mist started to fall and the sky darkened, but Maggie's floral perfume brought a sense of springtime to the dismal day.

He touched her hand. "Thanks for checking the back-room at Wally's."

"As cautiously as Bubba was guarding that room, I thought for sure he was trying to hide something."

"You didn't see anything unusual?"

"Nothing except a lot of clutter."

"No potbellied earthenware figures like the photo downloaded to your sister's computer?"

"Bubba can't keep a secret, can he?"

Maggie had acted heroically and her initiative had caused the pawnshop clerk to reveal his hand. LeShawn's attempt to deflect attention away from Bubba had been telling, as well. Without doubt, the earthenware figurine played into whatever was being shipped from Afghanistan, and both of the men were involved. But who else?

Leaving post through the main gate, Nate turned onto the road leading back to Freemont. The rain intensified, and he clicked on the windshield wipers.

Maggie glanced out the window. "God evidently listened to the prayers of the good people in Georgia."

He raised a brow. "How's that?"

She pointed to the standing water and overflowing sewers they passed. "How many people begged the Lord to end the years of drought? God evidently responded."

"I don't think they prayed for floods."

"But they prayed for rain, and God always gives us more than we ask for."

"Do I notice a bit of skepticism in your voice?"

She shook her head. "Not really. Things began to make sense a few months ago when I started going back to church."

"The world's still messed up, Maggie. Lots of folks have problems."

"You're right, but I feel better knowing God's in control. That realization makes me want to be part of the solution when I reach out to others."

"Which you do in your counseling practice."

She turned thoughtful eyes to gaze at him. "I used to do it with my head. Now I'm trying to do it with my heart."

Nate's hands tightened on the wheel. A faint thread of understanding wove through him along with her words. Other investigations had been matters of intellect. He'd been doing his job. Putting the pieces together. Head knowledge. Common sense. This time, with Maggie, something deeper was involved.

He was attracted to her physically, but it was more than that. Maybe for once, he'd gone beyond the intellect to the heart of the matter and had seen a glimmer of hope, which was something he needed to ponder in the future.

Right now the funeral director waited and a tough job had to be tackled. Nate planned to stay with Maggie and help her with any decisions she needed to make.

Heart or intellect? He needed to guard both, especially when he was around Maggie.

The funeral director was sympathetic and Maggie remained strong throughout the process of arranging for her sister's burial. She chose a fitting resting spot near a grove of pecan trees as well as a marble headstone and concluded the arrangements in time to make the meeting she had scheduled with Chaplain Grant.

Nate drove her to the chaplain's office in the Main Post Chapel complex and waited in the lobby, giving Maggie time alone with the clergyman.

Jamison met Nate there.

"I thought it might be easier to talk privately here." Jamison pointed to a small room across the hall from the Chaplain's office. The area was usually reserved for counseling.

As soon as the two agents sat down, Jamison asked, "How's Maggie doing?"

"Amazingly well, really. She's got an internal strength that seems to be supporting her."

"It's got to be tough, but then you can relate."

Nate thought of Michael's funeral. "Yeah. Maybe."

After mentioning the dark-colored sedan and then recounting what had happened at Wally's Pawn, Nate said, "The local police are keeping an eye on Kendra's neighborhood, but I want you to contact the Postal Inspectors and the FBI. The pawnshop needs to be kept under constant surveillance as well as the post offices on the list uncovered in Major Bennett's quarters."

Jamison nodded. "Looks like Wally's serves as the collection point for all the shipped goods."

"My thoughts exactly." Nate rubbed his hand over his chin. "Kendra said she gave the packages to a guy named LeShawn. He was at the shop today, a tall African-American, mid-thirties. See what you can find out about him. Also Ronald Jones. He goes by Bubba."

Jamison jotted down the names before Nate continued. "I have a feeling Wally's dealing in stolen weapons on the side." He gave Jamison the serial number off the .45 caliber Bubba had shown him. "Run a trace and see whether the firearm's stolen. If it is, civilian law enforcement will have a reason to haul all of them in for questioning."

"Will do."

"Did you learn anything about Maggie's father or his suicide?" Nate asked.

"The archived report was brief. Lieutenant Colonel Bennett took his own life. The funeral was held at the Main Post Chapel, and he was buried in his family's plot in Wisconsin where he'd grown up."

"Any indication as to why he had committed suicide?"

"Nothing was in the record."

"What about Graham Hughes?" Nate asked.

"I contacted the cab company. No pickups anywhere near where Graham was staying last night. Nor is there a record of any cabs gaining entry to post within an hour each way of the time of death."

"That still doesn't rule out the estranged husband."

"We talked to a second contractor who works with AmeriWorks. He said Graham keeps his nose clean and his eyes off the women."

"But he could have been hiding his philandering. After all, he was at Wanda's all night."

Jamison tapped his pencil against his notepad. "Seems to me someone would be talking if he was a womanizer."

"What about Arnold Zart?"

"I spoke with him at length. He's not real quick on the uptake, but he said last night was the first time Graham had shown any interest in another woman."

"Which doesn't prove anything." Nate couldn't hide the frustration in his voice.

"What's eating you?" Jamison followed his gaze across the hall to the closed door of the chaplain's office. "It's her, isn't it? I can see it, man. You're involved?"

"Involved?"

"Totally over the top. She gets to you." Jamison spread his hands. "Although I can't blame you. She's beautiful. Plus the pain she's going through gives her a certain vulnerability. Guys like that."

"I'm not any guy."

"No, you're not. You're a dedicated special agent who usually has great vision and believes in the Uniform Code of Military Justice." Jamison shook his head. "But nothing points to foul play in this case."

"Unless the connection between Major Bennett and whatever's being brought into the U.S. via the mail led someone to set up a murder to look like suicide."

"Guilt over her involvement in criminal activity could be what *caused* her suicide," Jamison suggested.

"What if she could have stumbled onto the operation and was killed to keep quiet?"

"The house was clean, Nate. No prints. No forced entry. No signs of a struggle."

"Have the alcohol and toxicology screens come back yet?"

"Blood alcohol was consistent with having consumed one to two glasses of wine. Still awaiting tox results."

Nate thought of the bottle of cabernet on the kitchen counter. "There were two wineglasses. Mills said the one in the dishwasher had been wiped clean of prints. Tell me, why would Major Bennett wipe down a glass she was going to wash?"

When Jamison failed to reply, Nate supplied the answer. "Because someone else wiped it down. Someone who drank wine with her that night. The same person wiped his prints off the bottle, as well. And who would Major Bennett let into her home? Who would know enough about her family history to set the stage for the suicide in just that way?"

"You think it has to be Graham Hughes?"

Nate leaned back into the chair. He glanced, once again, at the chaplain's office. "I don't know what to think."

Maggie was convinced Graham had killed her sister. Was she influencing Nate? Jamison was right. The evidence didn't seem to point to murder. But all the evidence wasn't in yet.

"What about her shoes?" Nate asked. "Did they dust them for prints?"

Jamison glanced through the file he'd pulled from his briefcase. "Not that I can see."

"I'm driving Maggie to Major Bennett's quarters as soon as she finishes talking to the chaplain. She needs to pick out the major's uniform for burial. I'll bag the shoes and bring them back to headquarters."

"I could notify Mills and have him stop by the house."

Nate shook his head. "Not a problem. I'll handle it."

Jamison hesitated, his lips pursed. "I hate to tell you, but Chief Wilson is ready to get this investigation wrapped up."

"It's been less than twenty-four hours."

"I know, but Sergeant Thorndike overheard a conversation the provost marshal had with the commanding general."

"The old man was putting pressure to bear?"

"Evidently."

"Thorndike talks too much."

"I'm just telling you what he told me." Jamison

checked his watch and then grabbed his briefcase. "I need to get back to headquarters and make those calls you requested."

A few minutes after Jamison left, the chaplain's door opened. A sense of relief washed over Nate. Maggie appeared calm and seemingly at peace, despite her puffy eyes. Evidently, she'd shed tears with Chaplain Grant. Hopefully they were cathartic.

Returning to her sister's home would be difficult. Nate was glad he could be with her to offer support, but when he pulled to a stop in front of Quarters 1448, his cell phone rang.

He glanced down at the caller ID before he raised the cell to his ear. "Kelly, give me a second." He turned to Maggie. "I'm sorry, but this won't take long."

"You go ahead and talk, Nate. I'll go inside."

"Are you sure?"

She nodded. Her eyes were clear, and the look of resolve on her face reassured him. "When you're through talking to Kelly, you can help me with Dani's uniform."

"You've still got the key to her quarters?"

Maggie nodded as she climbed from the car.

He watched her walk toward the house. Arranging for her sister's burial seemed to have given Maggie a feeling of usefulness despite her grief.

Nate returned the phone to his ear. "Sorry to keep you waiting, Kel."

"I'm driving through Atlanta and thought you might want me to stop by Fort Gillem."

He smiled. "To hustle our forensic lab along? Yeah, thanks. The blood alcohol came back, but I need the tox report. There's a rumor that Chief Wilson wants the case wrapped up ASAP, but I want to make sure we have all the facts in first."

"Sounds pretty straightforward from what I've heard," Kelly said before she disconnected. Like everyone else, she had an opinion about the case. Suicide was the option of choice, except Maggie was convinced her sister had been murdered. And now she had Nate starting to wonder.

Had Graham Hughes returned to the quarters and killed the major, as Maggie believed? If the major hadn't taken her own life and if Graham hadn't killed her, then who else would want the major dead?

Was there something else happening here that Nate hadn't yet figured out? Something that had put Major Bennett in harm's way and had led to her death?

Something that now placed others in danger?

SEVEN

Maggie stepped into the cool interior of Quarters 1448, all too aware she had found her sister's body the last time she'd come through that very same door. For a moment, she wished she had remained in the car with Nate, but he was busy with a phone call, and she didn't need to be a burden. He'd already done so much to support her throughout the day.

A momentary sense of calm filled her when she thought of his crystal-blue eyes and the compassion she read in his gaze. The man had a heart. Something she hadn't expected from a military officer, especially someone involved in law enforcement.

Moving into the living room, she noticed the curtains had been drawn, casting the interior of the home in shadow. Just as it had last night—actually early this morning—her gaze locked on her father's medals. The Bronze Star, the Meritorious Service Medal—others she couldn't name which he had worn with pride. As a child, she had thought he had placed more emphasis on the medals than he had his daughters.

Maggie, being more of an introvert, hadn't sought the attention Dani demanded. With black hair, expressive eyes and an energetic personality, Dani had made her presence known at every opportunity. In contrast, Maggie preferred to huddle in the corner with a book, living vicariously through the stories she read.

Not that either girl had been able to pull their less-than-demonstrative father from his job. Long workdays left little time to interact with his children. A fact of life Maggie accepted.

If anything, their father's aloofness coupled with their mother's illness forced the two sisters to depend on one another. Until—

Once again, tears swamped her eyes, like a cresting river ready to overflow its banks. Maggie counseled the grieving but was at a loss as to how to ease her own pain now. Time would help, she knew that much.

Life would get better if she lived in the moment and didn't try to anticipate the future. She'd done that today with Nate's help. Preparing for Dani's funeral had given her a sense of purpose for which she was grateful.

Pulling a tissue from her purse, she wiped the tears from her cheeks and inhaled deeply, fighting to gain control of her frayed emotions. She had a uniform to retrieve, which needed to be delivered to the funeral director.

With renewed determination, she grasped the banister and climbed the steps, wishing she and Dani could have had more time together. Here in her sister's home, Maggie could almost hear her laughter. Not that she could recall Dani laughing on the phone last night. Her voice had been tense and filled with apprehension.

Stepping onto the upper landing, Maggie tried to focus on the bedroom. Instead her gaze strayed to the attic door, hanging open like a giant cavern of pain and darkness. A lump lodged in Maggie's throat and brought more stinging tears to burn like salt water in her eyes.

Grabbing the knob to the master suite, she pushed into the room and away from the terrible memories of last night that played with her mind. A shuffle came from the built-in closet. She turned toward the sound and startled when a man stepped forward.

"Graham!"

He stared at her with that same cocky attitude that had girls flocking around him in high school. Including her. Although taller and broader, his appeal hadn't diminished. "Good to see you, Maggie."

"How dare you come back here." A fire ignited in the pit of her stomach, stoked by the smirk he plastered on his square face. "How can you have the gall to come back to the place where you killed my sister?"

His face twisted. "I didn't kill her. I loved her."

"You killed Dani and then spent the night with another woman. I don't call that love. I call it sick, disgusting."

"You have to let me explain." He stepped closer. "You've *never* allowed me to explain—not any of it."

She held up her hands, palms out, willing him to stop. The air thickened, and she suddenly couldn't breathe. A vision of her sister's body, hanging from the rafters, swirled through her mind.

"Maggie, you've got to understand—"

"Understand what? That you lied to every woman who ever cared for you? That you can't be trusted? That you only think of yourself and never of anyone else?"

"I've thought about you."

For half a heartbeat, she was once again that teenage

girl enamored with her sister's boyfriend. Then he took another step.

"Stay away from me, Graham."

His voice softened. "That's not what you said years ago."

She remembered all too well the things she had told him—foolish words that should never have been spoken.

"Don't, Graham." Her breath came in ragged gulps. She backed into the corner of the room, before realizing she could go no farther.

"There was a reason for everything that happened, Maggie."

She steeled herself to the velvet tone of his voice and fisted her hands. "You mean there's a reason why you killed Dani?"

"I did no such thing." His tone was emphatic.

"You killed her and made her death look like a suicide. I found her, just the way my mother found my father. You planned it that way, didn't you? You wanted to get back at me."

"Are you feeling guilty, Maggie?"

"Why would I feel guilty when you killed her?"

"I'm not talking about Dani." He reached for her hand. "Why didn't you tell anyone the truth about that night?"

Maggie jerked away. "What would I tell them? That I'd made a terrible mistake? Right after that the dominos started to fall. Dani got in trouble and then my father's death."

"You weren't to blame, baby."

"Don't call me that."

The bedroom door burst open. Nate stormed into the

room, gun drawn and aimed at Graham. "Back away from her."

Graham turned. "What the—"

"Now," Nate demanded.

Letting out a frustrated groan, Graham backed up toward the closet.

Nate glanced at Maggie, his face washed with concern. "Did he hurt you?"

She shook her head. "I…I'm okay."

He flicked his gaze back to Graham. "What are you doing here, Mr. Hughes?"

"Getting some of my things. You can talk to Jamison Steele. He told me that I could retrieve my personal items. Besides, I've got an alibi for last night."

"Yeah," Maggie spit out. "Another woman."

"Grab what you need, Mr. Hughes, and then leave the quarters immediately."

Graham stared first at Maggie and then at Nate as if deciding whether to comply. Finally, he pulled a few items from the dresser and stomped out of the room. His footfalls were heavy on the steps as he retreated downstairs and left through the back door. The sound of a car engine could be heard from the rear alley.

Maggie had felt confusion before, but now she was even more twisted inside. Tears streamed down her cheeks, clouding her eyes and making it impossible for her to see Nate. His strong arms wrapped around her. Folding into his embrace, she found his shoulder, soaking in the strength of him.

She needed him, needed his stability and levelheadedness, all the things that made him so opposite Graham. Nate stood for reason and righteousness. He was a good and honorable man.

What did he see when he looked at her? Did he see the mixed-up woman who had made bad choices with lasting repercussions? She had to keep the truth about who she was from Nate, no matter how much she wanted to bare her soul and tell him about the teenage girl who had fallen in love with her sister's boyfriend. All Maggie had wanted was someone to love. She'd never considered how her actions would change her family forever.

Nate felt Maggie's heart pounding against his chest. Her tears dampened his shirt, and her breath fanned his neck between her gut-wrenching sobs. He rubbed his fingers over her back, drawing her closer.

The very fiber of his being was tuned to Maggie's need, and at this moment, nothing else mattered except keeping her safe. His cheeks caressed her hair, like strands of gold mixed with spun silk. He inhaled, smelling her flowery perfume and the clean scent of shampoo.

A sense of his own manliness swelled within him, a sensation filled with so many emotions—righteousness coupled with mercy, virtue armored with strength. For the first time, he had a glimpse into his soul and was surprised by the goodness he found amassed there.

With Maggie in his arms, he felt invincible. Not in a worldly puffed-up way, but as a just warrior who battled evil and turned wrong to right. The power of those thoughts made him heady and mystified by the effect Maggie had on him.

"It's okay, honey," he soothed.

His fingers caressed her neck and tangled in her thick hair. "I'm here. No one's going to hurt you."

"Oh, Nate," she whispered.

What was happening to his ordered world? Right now, it was swirling out of control, but instead of crashing into destruction, he was being raised to something wonderful and larger than himself—larger than both of them.

Slowly, Maggie's sobs subsided. She pulled back slightly and stared into his eyes, searching his face. All rational thought left him, and he was aware of only the sweetness of her lips and how much he wanted to caress them with his own.

He lowered his mouth to meet hers.

The trill of his cell phone filled the breath of space between them. Maggie broke away from his embrace, sending his world toppling into confusion. For a matter of seconds, he couldn't move.

Her eyes, big as the universe just a moment ago had once again clouded. "Better answer that call." Her voice was husky with emotion.

Nate groped for his cell.

"Jamison, your timing couldn't be worse," Nate wanted to shout into the phone when he recognized the caller ID. Instead he listened as the agent talked about the surveillance that law enforcement had established around Wally's Pawn.

When they disconnected, Nate jammed his phone back in his pocket. Maggie stood with her arms around her waist, looking vulnerable and exposed. They'd gotten too close. She had to have felt it as much as he had.

Turning away from him, she opened one of the drawers, sifting through her sister's things. "I don't know where anything is." She changed the focus from what had just happened to the task of gathering clothing for her sister's burial.

Nate walked to the closet and pulled out the major's dress blue uniform, which he laid on the bed next to the small tote bag Maggie was quickly filling. Whether the funeral director needed all she packed was debatable, but Maggie felt useful and that was important.

She rummaged once again in the chest of drawers and found a small leather-bound book, which she pulled out and then flipped through.

"Something special?" he asked.

"A Bible." Her voice signaled surprise. Turning the pages, she eventually stopped and silently read a passage. Tears filled her eyes once again.

She pulled in a ragged breath and shook her head as if deeply moved by what she had read. "Over lunch, my sister talked about trying to get her life together. She mentioned her search for God. I…I had told her to turn to scripture."

Maggie looked at him as if seeking approval. If it relieved some of the sorrow he currently saw written so plainly on her face, he'd do anything to help, even agree with her that a passage in scripture had influenced her sister. He'd also escort Maggie to Sunday services in the morning, if that's what she wanted. He would do anything for her, except pull her back into his arms again, no matter how much he longed to do just that.

His recent show of affection had taken advantage of her vulnerability. He couldn't prey on her loneliness and pain. What had happened between them was colored by the situation and not from any real interest on her part.

Following the funeral, Maggie would leave Fort Rickman, which he knew held memories the beautiful counselor would probably want to shut out of her life.

When she shut out the memories, she'd shut him out, as well.

"I think we have everything," he said. "Why don't you keep the Bible if it brings you comfort."

She clutched it to her chest and nodded. He grabbed the uniform and the tote bag and held the bedroom door open for her. With her back ramrod straight and the Bible clutched in her hands, Maggie walked rapidly to the top of the stairwell, never glancing at the attic door that still hung open.

Nate closed it as he passed, then followed Maggie down the stairs. He hadn't questioned her about the run-in with Graham. There would be time for that later when her emotions weren't so raw.

Right now he wanted to get her back to Kelly's BOQ. Maggie looked exhausted. Dark lines circled her eyes and her cheeks were splotched from the tears she had cried. She probably had not slept much last night and stress had, no doubt, drained whatever reserve she had.

At the bottom of the stairs, Nate stopped and searched for the major's shoes, but couldn't find them. Evidently Corporal Mills had picked them up after all. He would check with Jamison when he got back to headquarters, after he dropped Maggie off at the BOQ and delivered the major's uniform to the funeral director.

On the way outside, Maggie opened the metal mailbox that hung next to the front door.

"Anything?" he asked.

"Just some junk mail." Her voice was flat and devoid of emotion as she pulled out the flyers.

The sooner he could get her away from the house, the better. He'd made a mistake bringing her here. He should have picked up the uniform without Maggie, but she had insisted on doing everything for her sister. He understood that need and remembered his desire to feel useful when Michael had died. Although he hadn't been able to do anything to wipe away his own guilt. That was the harsh reality of what had happened eight months ago. Something Nate would live with for the rest of his life.

He looked at Maggie standing on the porch and sorting through the advertisements, and a wave of regret washed over him. If only they had met under different circumstances, he and Maggie might have had a chance to build a relationship of trust. As it was now, he would always be the special agent who had let her down when it came to investigating her sister's death.

EIGHT

Placing the major's uniform on the backseat, Nate rounded his car to the passenger side and opened the door for Maggie, who was still sorting through the mail. He glanced down, then stooped lower to examine the two-inch gash in his rear tire.

The sound of a car engine distracted his attention. He stood as a military police sedan pulled to a stop. Sergeant Thorndike rolled down his window and scratched his graying hair.

"Looks like you've got a problem, sir."

An understatement for sure.

"Need some help?" the sergeant asked.

"Thanks, but I can handle it. Did you see anyone who looked suspicious when you entered the housing area?"

"I passed Mills on my way here. He mentioned seeing the Foglio kid." Thorndike pointed to the brick quarters across the street. "I thought I saw him hanging out down the block. Decided I'd talk to his dad and see if he was behaving himself."

Maggie shoved the mail into her purse and approached the car. Thorndike glanced her way, then at Nate. "I'd be happy to drive Ms. Bennett back to her motel, sir."

"She's staying at Agent McQueen's BOQ. I'll take her there after I change the tire, which won't take long. You pay the Foglios a visit, and see if anyone remembers anything more about last night, or if anyone was hanging around my car just now."

"The boy's dad claimed he was asleep when Major Bennett was killed. At least that's what he told Mills. I'll let you know if the story changes."

Nate made short work of the tire and had settled Maggie into the front of his car when Sergeant Thorndike exited the quarters across the street.

Approaching Nate, he said, "Mrs. Foglio's at home. She said Kyle has been helping her inside with chores."

"But you saw him on the corner?"

"Sure thought it was him, sir. The boy's the spitting image of his real mom, and that gal was trouble. She kept complaining her husband was up to no good, but she was the one with the problem."

"You know the other Mrs. Foglio?"

"Only by reputation. I was stationed with Foglio a long time ago when he was a general's aide and married to the first Mrs. Foglio. She was a gossip and always talked behind her husband's back. Said he was vindictive and mean. Not that anyone believed her. Glad to see the lieutenant colonel's done better the second time around. The current Mrs. Foglio seems nice enough, although I had the feeling she was covering up for her stepson today."

Or maybe Thorndike saw what he wanted to see. The teen had given the sergeant a hard time last summer. Thorndike could hold a grudge. Of course, there always was the possibility that the kid truly was trouble. Kelly had been suspicious of the boy, as well.

The teen had gone to stay with his mom after leaving last summer, but he had returned to Fort Rickman just a few days ago. Nate didn't believe in coincidences, yet he could see no connection between the major's death and Kyle Foglio being on post. In this case, the two seemingly random events were probably just that.

As Thorndike drove away, Nate's eyes settled on Maggie, waiting in the front seat of his car. She had dropped her head into her hands, and the pitiful spectacle of her continuing grief cut into him like a razor blade.

Why didn't you tell anyone the truth about that night? The accusation Graham had hurled at Maggie circled through Nate's memory.

What was she holding back? If it had a bearing on the major's death, Nate needed to know. No matter what, he wanted to help her.

Nate let out a long sigh, realizing he wanted to do more than help. He wanted to hold her close as he had done upstairs. Only this time, he would never let her go.

Maggie remained silent as Nate drove her back to Kelly's BOQ. He promised to drop off Dani's things at the funeral home before he returned to CID Headquarters for another briefing. Once inside the apartment, Maggie headed straight to bed. After what seemed like hours of tossing and turning, she finally dozed off but woke with a start later that evening when the phone rang.

She hurried into the living area and picked up the receiver. "Hello?"

Silence and then a dial tone.

She hung up.

Her stomach growled and propelled her to the kitchen. Her options included a lunch meat sandwich or the pizza Kelly said she could order by phone and have delivered.

Outside a car door slammed. Maggie edged back the kitchen curtain and peered through the window into the darkening night. Nate's car sat parked under a street-light. As she watched, he stepped onto the pavement and headed toward the BOQ complex.

Her pulse quickened. Needing Nate's support, she had thrown herself into his arms at Dani's quarters. Actually Maggie had needed him to protect her from the memories that had surfaced after seeing Graham. If Nate hadn't been there—

She shook her head. No reason to look back.

The door to Nate's BOQ closed, and she peered outside once again. This time she saw only the empty walkway.

The phone in the living room rang, and her heart rate picked up a notch. She grabbed the receiver and tried to control the enthusiasm bubbling up within her.

"Hi, Nate." A smile circled her lips but quickly disappeared in response to the silence that greeted her.

"Hello?"

Someone pulled in a deep breath.

"Who is this?"

When no one answered, she slammed the receiver back on the cradle and punched in *-6-9 to retrieve the caller's phone number. Either the post phone service didn't provide the service or the call had come from an untraceable number.

Maggie's frustration subsided, replaced with an eerie sense of foreboding. Silly, she knew, but she was in a strange apartment and so much had happened. She lowered the blinds in the living area and debated calling her special agent neighbor. As much as she should stay away from Nate, she also needed to focus on something other than her sister's death and the memories of the past, which included Graham Hughes.

Nate had to be tired. He didn't need her underfoot, and he probably had a girlfriend. Then she thought of what had happened this afternoon. His breath had been as ragged as hers, and the electricity that had passed between them gave no evidence of anyone else in his life.

Of course, the moment had been an accidental encounter when he had sensed her need for comfort. Nothing more, she told herself as she combed her hair and refreshed her makeup. Looking into the guest room mirror, she laughed. Who was she trying to kid? The guy got to her, in a good way. If she spent a little time in his company tonight, she'd be able to get her thoughts off her problems.

Her stomach growled again. Plus, she was hungry.

Maybe Nate would like to share a pizza. With that in mind, she hurried to his door and knocked. When he answered, with his tie undone and shirt partially unbuttoned, she struggled to breathe.

"Maggie?"

His surprise took her aback. Had he been expecting someone else?

She glanced into the neatly furnished BOQ. "Am I disturbing anything?"

"I was thinking of throwing a couple steaks on the grill and was about to call you. I thought you might be hungry."

So he *was* thinking of her.

Maggie smiled as she stepped into his apartment, feeling a sense of rightness. The soothing notes of a solo sax filled the room. A couch and matching chair in earth tones surrounded a square coffee table on which sat a stack of books and a framed five-by-seven photograph. As Maggie neared, she gazed at the picture of Nate in the camouflaged army combat uniform with his arm slung over the shoulder of a younger version of himself dressed in similar military attire.

Large grins were plastered on both faces as if the two men shared a joke no one else understood. Perhaps, she reasoned, their levity had to do not only with a familial brotherhood, which would explain their similar features, but also their shared love of the military.

She pointed to the photo. "Your brother?"

"Michael." The single-word response held both pride and pain.

She waited for Nate to provide more information. When he didn't, she took in the rest of the room with a quick glance. A bookcase filled with military texts hugged the far wall opposite the state-of-the-art sound system and a flat-screen TV. A high-tech computer sat perched on a desk in the corner.

"You like technology." She hoped her statement would turn the focus away from the photograph.

"Just a geek at heart." He smiled, sending a flutter to her midsection and relief that he'd moved beyond the seemingly raw emotion he still carried concerning his brother's death.

She and Dani had only started to reunite after years of being estranged. As significant and good as that coming together had been, Maggie had survived for years without having Dani in her life. Nate, on the other hand, appeared to have had a strong attachment to his little brother. He had mentioned eight months having passed since the young man's death. Maggie thought back to her father's death. Sixteen years and the wound still gaped open at times.

Nate motioned her toward the kitchen. "I was going to make a salad. There's French bread plus fresh strawberries for dessert."

Maggie licked her lips, causing Nate to laugh.

"Join me," he said, placing his hand on her arm and walking her into the small, cozy kitchen where the smell of sautéed garlic and onions teased her senses.

She inhaled deeply. "Makes me think I'm on a cooking show." She raised her brow, teasing. "Cooking with Nate?"

"A bachelor has to eat. Plus, I like mushrooms with my steak." He tossed fresh Portobellos into the garlic-onion mix.

"May I help with something?"

"Lettuce is in the fridge. If you're so inclined, I'll leave the salad to you."

She opened the refrigerator and reached for the plastic bag filled with washed greens, noting the milk and orange juice, an egg carton, deli lunch meat and an assortment of cheese and condiments. On a lower shelf, two steaks marinated. A refrigerator told a lot about a man. This one screamed neat and organized. No excess. No waste.

"Tomatoes and cucumbers are in the bottom crisper drawer," he said.

She placed both on the counter where he had laid a carving board and knife next to a wooden salad bowl. A small wrought-iron table with two chairs sat in the corner nook set for two.

Maybe she *had* interrupted his Saturday night plans.

"Looks like you were expecting company."

"I told you, I planned to see if you were hungry."

"That's very thoughtful of you, Nate. Thank you."

With one hand on the open refrigerator door and the other reaching for the steaks, he glanced back at her and winked. "I'm a nice guy, Maggie."

His smile was disarming, and her cheeks flushed with warmth. As always, she regretted her fair skin that revealed so much about what she was feeling.

Right now she was feeling at home with the handsome warrant officer. Although the longer he continued to stare at her, the more she struggled to keep her expression neutral. Inside, she felt like Match Light charcoal ready to burst into flame.

Nate turned back to the meat he had pulled from the fridge. "Fire's ready. My jacket's in the living room. Slip it on, if you feel like joining me outside."

Maggie reached for the navy blazer and draped the lightweight wool over her shoulders. The smell of Nate's aftershave swirled around her, filling her with a sense of comfort and security. Nate proved to be accomplished with the grill and before long the steaks were on the table, and she was sitting in the chair he held for her.

"Everything looks and smells delicious. I haven't had a decent meal in…" She tried to think back but got stuck on what had happened to her sister.

Nate seemed to pick up on her struggle and directed her down a different path. "It's nice to have someone to eat with for a change."

"You and Kelly don't get together for potlucks?"

"Occasionally. Although we often work different shifts. Kel is a great investigator, but our relationship is purely professional, if that's what you were asking."

Maggie hadn't intended to ask anything about their relationship and had only thought about two single people finding friendship after a long day at work. Although she felt a glow of pleasure, learning the two special agents weren't involved. Not that she should be interested in Nate in any way except as an officer of the law, looking into her sister's death. But the man did something to her equilibrium, especially when his blue eyes stared at her as they were doing now, upping her internal thermostat and making her skin pink even more.

She dropped the napkin onto her lap and lowered her head, saying her own private blessing, hoping to calm her flushed skin with a thankful word to the Lord. When she glanced up, Nate was still staring at her, sending more sparks coursing through her veins. At this rate, she'd be charbroiled before the meal was over.

"So you and God are tight?" He reached for his fork, evidently aware of the prayer she'd offered for both herself and Nate.

Recalling the ambiguous comments regarding faith he had made the night before, Maggie weighed whether she should step through the door he seemed to have cracked open. Her counselor side couldn't resist the opportunity to find out more about his psychological as well as spiritual wounds and won the toss.

"Did your brother's death derail your relationship with God?" She stabbed a bite of salad to diffuse the impact of her question.

"There wasn't much to ruin."

"When we were with Chaplain Grant last night, you said it was hard to trust a loving God when your world fell apart. Michael's death must have affected you deeply."

He broke off a hunk of French bread and slathered it with butter. "His death affected a number of things in my life, including the way I look at God."

"God doesn't want you to be in pain, Nate. You know that, don't you?"

He raised his brow and smiled, a hint of embarrassment evident in the curl of his lips. "For some reason, I feel like I'm undergoing counseling."

"Sorry. Force of habit." She smiled back, realizing Nate had sidestepped the issue at hand. Then, trying to cover the awkwardness, she changed the subject to the saxophone player whose music filtered softly into the kitchen. The steak smelled delicious, and she dug into the meat, feeling ravenous, which was a good sign.

Their conversation moved from music to bestselling books and eventually movies they'd both seen. They kept the tone light so nothing could bring them back to either Dani's or Nate's brother's deaths. Later, as they sipped coffee and ate the plump strawberries Nate served with a dollop of yogurt on top, they ran out of safe topics.

Nate fiddled with the napkin he had tossed on the

table. His body language screamed he had something on his mind.

"Church services at the Main Post Chapel are at 11:00 a.m.," he finally said. "If you'd like to attend tomorrow, I could drive you."

"And pick me up afterward, as well?"

"I'll attend the service *with* you, Maggie."

"Despite your feelings?"

"Yes, despite my feelings." He held up his hand, palm out. "And no more questions. I'll handle my relationship with God. You let me know if you'd like to go to church."

"I would. Thank you."

He took a sip of coffee and eyed her over the rim of his mug as if something else needed to be said. Finally, he sighed. "You heard the chaplain mention two men who were killed in Afghanistan a few days ago?"

How could Maggie have forgotten? "The men in Dani's unit?"

"That's right. One of the men was from New Jersey, as the chaplain said. The other man was a company commander in your sister's unit. His body is being flown back to Fort Rickman tomorrow. The unit will be there to pay him honor as his remains are taken off the aircraft and transported to the funeral home we visited today."

She waited for him to continue.

"After church, I'll drive you back to Kelly's BOQ. But I wanted you to know where I'd be in the afternoon."

"If the public is invited, Nate, I'd like to honor the fallen commander, as well. The least I can do is to pay my respects." She rubbed her finger over the lip of her mug. "And represent my sister. I…I think she'd want that."

Nate nodded as if he understood. "I hoped you would feel up to it. The ceremony is as heartwarming as it is heart wrenching. The honor paid to the remains, the support of the men, standing in formation…well, it makes you realize the cost of war."

"I never underestimate the price some people have to pay in service to our country." She paused for a moment and then added, "Your brother, for instance. It must have been hard on your parents."

Nate looked down at the table and brushed crumbs into his hand. When he spoke his voice was raw with emotion. "They never talk about him when we're together, which I must admit, isn't often."

Maggie stared at him, knowing full well she was looking through a counselor's eye, but also that she was beginning to care about this military man with the wounded heart.

"Are they more concerned, perhaps, about the son who survived?" she asked.

His eyes captured hers, surprise written on his face. "Meaning?"

"Meaning your mom and dad might fear talking about Michael is too troubling for *you* to handle."

He shook his head. "That's ridiculous. I deal with death cases as a CID agent on a regular basis. I was in Afghanistan for more than a year, Maggie. Death was a way of life there."

"But the other men weren't family."

"Not family, but there's a camaraderie in the military that civilians don't understand. We're united in our common purpose and our allegiance to the flag and to this nation. That bond is like a brotherhood."

"But no matter how strong the military bond is, Michael was your flesh-and-blood brother. From the looks of the picture you keep on your coffee table, your relationship was close. My guess is Michael idolized his big brother and considered you his hero."

Nate scooted his chair back and stood. "I'm not a hero."

"Of course you are. You served in a war zone. You've dedicated yourself to serving your country. That makes you a hero by default."

"I told you." She hadn't expected the intensity in his voice. "I'm not a hero. I've made mistakes. Big ones."

"Everyone makes mistakes, Nate. No one is perfect."

"Yeah, but some mistakes cost more dearly than others."

Maybe it was her years of helping people expose their internal wounds, but she could see beneath the anger. If only Nate would allow her to lead him into the pain he tried to cover over, maybe she could help him begin to heal. She wondered if he gave himself permission to reflect on what had happened and the role he had played.

Too often painful events were pushed aside or buried in the past, where they festered like an abscess hidden deep within the body. Eventually the infection would surface.

Had Nate buried the memory of his brother's death so deep that he ignored the pain it was causing? If only she could expose it to the light of day and find the truth about what had happened eight months ago. If he was at fault, he needed to ask God's forgiveness and then forgive himself. Only then would he be healed.

Whether he realized it or not, Nate displayed classic

symptoms of guilt. He felt responsible for his brother, more than likely, because the younger sibling had followed him into the military. That alone could weigh heavily on anyone's shoulders. But there was something else that cut deeper than failing to live up to a brother's adulation.

"What happened, Nate, that makes you feel responsible for your brother's death?"

He stared at her, his jaw firm.

"It's more than Michael wanting to follow in your footsteps, isn't it?" She continued to push. "There's a deeper issue you haven't been able to tell anyone."

The pulse point on his temple thumped. His hands fisted, and his lips clamped shut. He looked at her, but she knew he didn't see her. He was seeing what had happened in Afghanistan.

She lowered her voice. "Were you there when he died?"

He shook his head.

"But you think there's something you could have done to have prevented it." She said it as a statement and the narrowing of his gaze proved she'd zeroed in on exactly how he felt.

"I...I shouldn't have believed him."

Maggie didn't understand the last comment, but if she let Nate talk, the truth would come out.

"Michael was young and too naive for his own good."

She nodded, hoping Nate would continue.

Instead, he placed his cup in the sink and stood for a long moment before he asked, "Would you care for more coffee?"

The change of subject caught her off guard. "You've

got to face the problem one of these days, Nate, in order to heal."

"I'm fine, Maggie."

"No you're not. You're carrying the guilt of your brother's death all alone."

"And who can I share it with? You? You recognize my sin because you've got your own, don't you, Maggie?"

She tensed. "I don't know what you mean."

"I mean there's something you're keeping from me. Graham said as much today, but for some reason you can't trust me enough to tell me the truth."

"I…I trust you."

"Do you, Maggie? Then level with me. What's the secret?"

"I don't know what you're talking about."

"Yes, you do. It's written all over your face. Or maybe I can recognize it because I know about taking responsibility when a loved one dies."

"I didn't kill Dani. Her husband did."

"Graham's alibi holds up, Maggie."

"You believe the woman who spent the night with him? She's lying, Nate. Graham killed Dani when he returned to their quarters late last night. Then he hung her body from the rafter to make her death look just like my father's suicide."

"But why would he do that, Maggie?"

"It has to do with what Dani uncovered in Afghanistan. She got too close to something and Graham had to find a way to stop her without making anyone suspicious." She trembled as the memory of Dani's death and her father's returned to haunt her. "The war, the deployment, fatigue and jet lag on the long flight back to the States added fuel to the fire so everyone would believe Dani had taken her own life."

Maggie pushed back her chair and stood. "You believe it was suicide. So does Jamison. Kelly probably does, as well. No one's looking deeper. No one's trying to uncover pieces of the puzzle that don't fit."

Nate stepped closer and reached out to capture a wayward strand of hair to tuck behind her ear. "What pieces of the puzzle do you hold, Maggie?"

She pulled back as if he'd burned her, knowing she had to get away from his piercing blue eyes that seemed to bore through her.

"Thanks for dinner, Nate. I'm suddenly very tired."

Without another comment, she hurried through the living room and out of his BOQ, wanting to distance herself from the special agent.

Entering Kelly's apartment, Maggie locked the door behind her. Tears rolled down her cheeks. Why couldn't she be stronger, like Dani had been? Why did she always have to be the quiet one who hid in the corner and never stood up for herself?

That's why her dad never seemed to notice her. Dani had said as much. Those hateful words about how their father didn't have time for Maggie because she was timid and unassuming.

Sixteen years and Dani's words still stung. Her sister hadn't been thinking when she'd hurled the comments at Maggie and attacked her with what Dani knew would hurt most. She had been reacting to her own pain. Rumors had circulated through school that day implying Graham was interested in someone else. Dani's fear of abandonment had sent her into a rage. Although she hadn't known who the other girl was, Dani had taken out her frustration on Maggie.

Her sister's actions had been bad enough, but then, Maggie had struck back. She had wanted to prove herself to her sister, prove that she had a backbone and could stand up for herself. But she'd gone too far, never realizing the terrible consequences for her actions that eventually led to their dad's suicide.

Nate wanted to know her secret. She couldn't tell him. She couldn't tell anyone.

He had mentioned that Maggie didn't trust him. The truth was she couldn't trust herself.

Besides, Nate should be focusing on Dani's murder instead of digging up painful memories that needed to remain buried in the past.

Wiping the tears from her cheeks she started toward the bedroom when the phone rang.

Nate?

Did she even want to talk to him? With another swipe at the tears, she lifted the receiver to her ear.

Silence. Then a pull of air and a low, maniacal chuckle. Someone was making fun of her.

"Who is this?"

"Spike."

The hair rose on her neck. She slammed the receiver back on the cradle, and her stomach roiled in protest. Why had she forgotten to mention the earlier hang-up call to Nate?

The phone rang again, sending a shiver up Maggie's spine. She raised the receiver to her ear.

"Graham, I know it's you. Don't call me again." She disconnected the phone from the wall and headed to bed.

Hopefully, she'd sleep.

But when she laid down, she wasn't surprised when sleep didn't come.

NINE

The next day Nate polished the brass insignia on his uniform, shined his shoes until he should see himself in the reflective leather and dressed for both the Sunday church service and the honor ceremony following.

On the way out of his quarters, he glanced at his reflection in the mirror, hoping he looked better than he felt. He'd been up for hours, thinking of everything that had happened with Maggie last night.

She had forced him to look back eight months. Even after all this time, the bottom line remained the same. He had been the one who had made the mistake, and that mistake had cost his brother's life. As long as he lived, Nate would always carry the heavy weight of responsibility on his own shoulders. He couldn't talk to his parents and was inclined to keep his distance. Whenever he went home, all he could see was Michael's face.

Checking that his medals were lined up perfectly on his chest, Nate grabbed his hat and walked across the stairwell to Kelly's door. He hadn't expected to have the wind knocked out of him when Maggie opened it, looking beautiful beyond words.

"Let me get my purse." Nate stepped inside, inhaling the sweet perfume that lingered after she moved down the hallway. The smell of freshly perked coffee mixed with the scent of shampoo and perfumed soap, filling the apartment with an uplifting bit of hope that spring would come despite the overcast February day.

Maggie's footfalls sounded from the hallway as she returned to join him. Nate readied himself for another jolt of adrenaline when she rounded the corner and stepped close. Her eyes were tired, but her smile lit up the room and warmed him despite the cool temperature outside.

She wore a navy dress with a matching jacket made of a soft, pliable material and had tied a gold paisley scarf around her neck that brought out the highlights in her hair.

He held the door for her and touched her back as he escorted her along the walkway toward his car. The sun tried to peer out from behind the clouds. For the family of the fallen soldier's sake, Nate hoped the rain would stay at bay so the honor guard ceremony could be performed without a glitch.

Once they were headed for the Main Post Chapel, Maggie turned to him. "You look very dashing in your uniform."

He hadn't expected the pinpricks that caused his neck to warm. "The CID routinely wears civilian clothes while covering an investigation. Today everyone wanted to look their best. Besides…" He smiled. "I wanted to keep up with you. Nice dress."

Her lips turned upward for a moment while her fingers played over the sleeve of her jacket. "When Dani called the other night, sounding so upset, I threw a few things in a suitcase, intending to spend the weekend. I packed this outfit to wear to church. You'll see me in it tomorrow for my sister's funeral."

"You look lovely."

She glanced down as if gathering her thoughts. "When I was talking to the Chaplain yesterday, he said he was able to get an eight-by-ten of Dani in uniform from her unit, but he suggested having an earlier picture from her childhood that would include my parents and me."

"Is that going to be a problem?"

She shook her head. "I don't think so. I called my neighbor while I was in the chaplain's office. She has a key to my place and promised to mail a photo I have of all of us. Dani was a sophomore and I had just started high school. The picture was taken…"

Maggie hesitated for a long moment. "It was taken when we first moved to Fort Rickman and before my father's death. I…I thought it might be good to include a memory of better times in the service."

"Is your neighbor bringing the photograph to the funeral?"

"She has to work, but she promised to mail it overnight express with a Sunday delivery. I wasn't sure about Kelly's address so I told my friend to send it to Dani's quarters."

"We can check later to see if the package arrived."

"Thanks, Nate."

They rode in silence for a few minutes, until Maggie asked, "Has the toxicology screen come back yet?"

He shook his head. "Unfortunately, no. Our forensic lab is located near Atlanta. Kelly stopped by yesterday on her way through the city, hoping to speed up the process. Might take a few more days before we get the results."

"I thought about it all last night. Graham must have drugged her."

Evidently Maggie hadn't been able to sleep, either.

"If Dani did have some wine, he could have slipped a sedative into her glass," Maggie continued. "Once she passed out, he carried her upstairs to the attic."

"But you said your sister didn't like wine."

"She'd never buy it herself—especially not red wine— but if Graham brought over the bottle, she wouldn't go so far as to refuse to have a glass with him. Graham knew that."

"Why wouldn't he just kill her downstairs? A man as strong as Graham could have strangled her or used his fists to incapacitate her. Why go to all the trouble to fake a suicide?"

"Because he didn't want to make her death draw any suspicion. Our dad's suicide would just make people think 'Like father, like daughter.' Plus Graham knew how important our father was to Dani. I told you that she idolized him and always tried to gain his attention. Anyone who didn't know her well enough to know how hurt she was by his actions might believe she'd choose to imitate him in that way."

Nate and Maggie seemed to go over the same threads of information each time they were together, yet they never wove the pieces together. Throughout the Sunday church service, Nate kept thinking about the threads that led nowhere instead of listening to Chaplain Grant's sermon. Maybe it was Nate's unease being in church, but the chaplain seemed less than exuberant in his praise for the Lord, probably because of what awaited him after the service.

The entire post was feeling the pain of the deaths. Counting the death of the soldier killed in the hunting accident that Kelly was investigating, the 2nd Transportation Battalion had lost four of its own in less than two weeks. That high of a casualty rate would place a pall on anyone, even a man of the cloth.

After the service, Nate drove with Maggie to the airfield on post. They passed a number of hangars and three helicopters parked on the nearby tarmac before he pulled into a parking spot and held the passenger door open as she stepped from the car. Taking her arm, he ushered her through the crowd of somber people to where a row of chairs reserved for the dignitaries had been placed near a podium, backdropped with the American flag. Across from the VIP area, the 2nd Transportation Battalion's rear detachment and various personnel who had been in the advance party stood in formation.

The sun peeked through the clouds, sending rays of light into the doleful day. Not even the sporadic brightness could lighten the tension in the crowd of onlookers who had gathered to pay their respects to the fallen company commander.

Nate checked his watch. "The plane is scheduled to land in ten minutes. The dignitaries should be taking their seats soon."

As if on cue, the side door to the nearest hangar opened and the post commanding general, chief of staff and command sergeant major stepped into the muted sunlight. Chaplain Grant followed, escorting a woman, probably mid-thirties, with two young children in tow.

She was dressed in a navy skirt, white blouse and red jacket. The children wore the same colors in patriotic matching plaids. The youngest child, an adorable tow-headed boy with big eyes, carried a small American flag that he waved as he walked across the tarmac beside his mother.

Nate tightened his jaw, steeling himself to the poignant reminder of the high cost of war. Maggie moaned under her breath, and he knew she had been affected by the widow and children, also.

"A yellow ribbon," Maggie whispered. The corsage and bow pinned to the woman's lapel were visible as she turned and hurried her children along.

Nate nodded, remembering all too well when he and his brother had left for Afghanistan. Their mother had tied a yellow ribbon around the oak tree in their front yard—the same tree the brothers had climbed as boys. Although faded, the ribbon was still in place the last time Nate had been home.

As if in unison, the crowd emitted a sigh of anticipation when a plane appeared in the distant sky. Nate glanced at Maggie to ensure she was okay, needing something to look at instead of the small family that watched the aircraft's approach for landing.

Maggie leaned into Nate. Her tired eyes held tears she blinked to keep at bay. Without forethought, he reached for her hand and their fingers entwined.

A state representative, the mayor of Freemont and the city manager took their places beside the fatherless family, followed by the chief of police, fire chief and a handful of city council members.

From the other side of the tarmac, the military band began to play a patriotic march that sounded almost too spirited for the soulful occasion. After the plane landed and taxied to a stop, the cargo hatch opened, and the honor guard marched up the ramp and into the belly of the craft.

A hush fell over the crowd, leaving only the cadenced footfalls of the soldiers to echo in the stillness of the day. With stoic faces, they carried the flag-draped casket onto the soil of the country the captain had loved so much. Passing in front of the wife and children, who stood with the other dignitaries, the honor guard placed the casket on the metal bier that had been prepared. In slow motion, they saluted the casket, paying tribute to their comrade in arms. Nate and the others in uniform followed suit.

The commanding general moved to the podium and addressed the crowd, highlighting Captain York's heroism and valor and the great loss his death was to his family, his unit and his country.

The chaplain replaced the general at the microphone for prayer. Maggie bowed her head and folded her hands. Nate lowered his gaze as the chaplain's words floated around them.

"Dear Father in Heaven, provide support for this strong woman and her two children in the days ahead. Comfort them as they mourn and allow them to know that her husband and their father was, indeed, one of America's finest heroes—a soldier, a leader, a commander, who put You, Lord, and this country first. Let peace reign not only in our hearts today but throughout the world because of the dedication to duty of our brave military and those special patriots who have made the ultimate sacrifice. Draw them into Your heavenly home and surround them with Your love. Amen."

At the conclusion of his prayer, the chaplain walked to the widow's side and encircled her with a supportive embrace, no doubt intoning his own private words of consolation before the state representative added his remarks about the fine man who had lost his life, protecting freedom.

Once the scheduled speakers had taken turns at the podium, the chaplain again returned to the microphone. "Mrs. York has asked to address you this morning." He turned and motioned her forward.

In a clear, strong voice, the attractive widow leaned into the microphone. "Mark would have been pleased to see so many people here. He also would have been humbled. As Chaplain Grant mentioned, my husband was a man who knew the Lord and loved Him above all things. He also loved his country and the men and women with whom he served. You honor him today, and in doing so, you honor our country, as well. Thank you, and God bless you all."

Tears rolled down Maggie's cheeks as the honor guard lifted the casket into the hearse. Nate and the other military in uniform saluted just before the chaplain escorted the family to the waiting limousine.

Nate pulled a handkerchief from his pocket and offered it to Maggie. "Thanks," she murmured, her voice husky with emotion. She dabbed at the moisture on her cheeks and allowed him to take her arm as they hastened back to his car.

The motorcade stretched for blocks. A police escort led the way with their lights flashing. Behind the family and dignities, a stream of military personnel and townspeople caravanned through the front gate of post and onto the main thoroughfare that headed toward the funeral home. All along the road, people stood with their hands over their hearts, watching in silence, their faces grief-stricken, as the sky darkened overhead.

"I had no idea of the outpouring of support the family would receive." Maggie stared at the throng of people, who stood motionless even as a light drizzle of rain began to fall.

Nate followed her gaze. "The good folks in this area of the country understand the sacrifice some are called to make."

"But surely Captain York isn't the first person from Fort Rickman to have lost his life?"

"Unfortunately there have been others, but the townspeople pay honor to every fallen soldier whose body is returned home. It's always poignant, and their support is heartfelt. The chaplain says the families find great comfort in the expression of sympathy."

"Did you...did you experience the same thing when your brother died?"

A lump jammed Nate's throat and prevented him from speaking, but his mind was sharp as he recalled how the people in his hometown had given Michael a hero's welcome just as Freemont had done for Captain York. They had also reached out to Nate and talked about his valor in combat. He hadn't wanted the kind words or the focus on himself. As he had told Maggie last night, Michael was the hero, not him.

Maggie touched his arm. "Are you okay, Nate?"

He nodded. That's all he could do. No matter how much he wanted to tell her about what had happened in Afghanistan, he couldn't. She was right. He carried the guilt of his brother's death because he had made a terrible mistake.

Nate could never forgive himself. Even harder to realize was that God couldn't forgive him, and if God couldn't forgive him, no one else could, either.

Not his parents.

Not Michael's girlfriend, Angela.

Not even Maggie, despite what she had said last night about the Lord not wanting to cause him pain.

Maggie sensed Nate's internal struggle. He had cracked open the door to his past last night. She needed to do the same. But nothing came easily these days, especially since her sister's death. Maggie had lived with the past sealed in the locked vault of her heart. If she could, she would have thrown away the key.

Seeing the confusion that shadowed Nate's eyes forced Maggie to break open the lock on her past. "For so long, I harbored resentment for the military because of everything that had happened after my father's death. In addition, my mother had been diagnosed with cancer a year earlier, and my family was still trying to adjust."

"That's got to be hard on a kid."

The empathy she heard in Nate's voice comforted Maggie and gave her the courage to continue. "My mother had participated in an experimental and expensive new treatment at a special cancer center in Texas for three months. She returned home, seemingly cured. At least that's what my father had told us."

As painful as the memories were, Maggie needed to tell Nate what she had faced. "After Dad died, we had to leave our home on post and move to Alabama. In what seemed like a swirl of grief and turmoil, we packed up our belongings and headed to a rural town, where we didn't know anyone. Dani was outgoing and made new friends easily. She joined the ROTC program at the high school and got involved. I remember my mother telling her that she'd made good choices."

Nate turned to gaze at her. "What about you, Maggie?"

"I was shy. Making friends was difficult. Looking back, I realize I should have gone to counseling, but that would have placed more of a stigma on our family. Or at least that's what my mother thought at the time."

"So you decided to become a therapist to help others just as you had needed help yourself?"

"And to dispel some of the misperceptions people have. Folks are more open now, but at that time in rural Alabama, I would have been seen as even more of an anomaly had I sought help."

"Could you talk to your mom about what you were feeling?"

Maggie shook her head. "Regrettably, we did everything as a family to mask our pain and tiptoed around the truth. Besides, my mother's cancer returned, no doubt brought on by the stress of losing her husband, so I never told her how isolated I truly felt."

Nate reached out and took Maggie's hand. She appreciated the warmth of his touch and the encouragement he offered in that small action.

When she spoke, her voice was a whisper. "I've always wanted to right all the wrongs that happened."

"Just like your sister."

Maggie nodded. "Maybe we weren't that different after all."

"My brother was eight years younger, but we were close." Biting his upper lip, Nate shook his head ever so slightly. "I thought about leaving town before his funeral and heading back to my unit. The wound of his death was still too raw, and I didn't think I could survive the comments made by so many."

"I know the feeling. Part of me wants to run away."

He turned to stare into her eyes. "But you can't, Maggie."

"That doesn't stop me from wishing I could."

"I guess not." He let out a ragged breath and refocused his gaze on the road. "Michael's girlfriend, Angela, was standing outside the church when my parents and I pulled into the parking lot the day of my brother's funeral. The soft swell to her belly was evident. I did the math from the two weeks when my brother had come home for R&R."

"Oh, Nate."

"Close as I could figure, Angela was five months along. My parents hadn't mentioned her pregnancy, and I realized they probably didn't know." He shook his head. "Silly kids. They hadn't thought about the consequences of their lovemaking. Nor had they realized their child would never get to know firsthand what a great guy Michael had been."

"At least, your brother died with honor." She pulled in a deep breath and glanced once again at the crowds lining the street. "Dani's funeral will be like my father's with the unspoken stigma of suicide hovering over the service."

"Chaplain Grant will ensure she's given a proper burial, Maggie."

"Hopefully, but it will be what he doesn't say that people will remember." She glanced at Nate, waiting to see if he would respond.

He squeezed her hand and then released it to make the next turn. "The truth will come out, Maggie."

"Maybe, but it seems to me everyone is blinded by what they want to see." Maggie shoved a strand of hair behind her ear and pursed her lips. "Doesn't it stand to reason that Dani may have been killed because of that list of names and post office boxes?"

"I notified the CID in Afghanistan. They're trying to track down information on that end. The Postal Inspection Service has the post offices under surveillance and the FBI's involved, but we need a break, something concrete that will change this to a murder case."

"What about Kendra's testimony? Isn't that enough to establish wrongdoing?"

"She's not a credible witness. I had the local police do a check. She's had a series of run-ins with the law."

"So you don't believe her because she has a past?"

"I never said that." He turned weary eyes toward Maggie. "I'm attempting to get to the truth, okay? But I need evidence. Something factual that I can take to my commander. Chief Wilson is convinced your sister took her own life. Nothing, including the autopsy, indicated she struggled. We're still waiting for the toxicology screen."

"There's something I didn't tell you." Maggie hesitated. "My sister said the military police were involved in whatever had happened in Afghanistan. The night before last, when you questioned me, I...I didn't know who could be trusted." She shook her head. "So much had happened."

He glanced at her, their eyes locking. "Can you trust me now?"

She nodded, confident she could share what Dani

had said. "My sister said that she had uncovered some type of an illegal operation in Afghanistan. She mailed evidence, as she called it, back to the States, to her quarters."

"Maybe one of the boxes Kendra talked about?"

"I don't know. Dani planned to take whatever it was to the provost marshal. She said he'd know what to do."

"The provost marshal is a good man."

He might be a good man, but Maggie needed him to be fair and impartial about her sister's death. Dani had tried so hard to redeem her father's memory. Now Maggie felt the need to do the same for Dani. As the lead investigator, surely Nate could influence others in the CID. Although at this point, Maggie wasn't sure what Nate actually believed.

Hopefully, something would happen to prove what she knew to be true. She thought of Kendra and her young daughter. Just so no one else would be hurt.

TEN

The police escort led the caravan to the funeral home. Nate parked and walked with Maggie to where the honor guard stood at attention. The funeral director opened the rear door of the hearse, and with the same uniform precision they had executed on the tarmac, the military detail removed the coffin and carried it inside.

With Captain York safely delivered to his destination, Nate and Maggie returned to his car, their clothing damp from the lightly falling mist.

Nate pulled onto the main road heading back to post. "I'll drop you off at Kelly's. Then I've got to stop by headquarters and contact the CID lab to find out if they've completed the toxicology screen. Plus there's a briefing with the provost marshal at 1600 hours. Four o'clock."

"Are you going to mention the evidence Dani mailed to her quarters?"

"I need to present all the information, Maggie."

"But what if it gets into the wrong hands?"

"Then we'll deal with whatever happens." Although he wouldn't voice his suspicions, Nate was concerned that Major Bennett's warning about law enforcement could have been to protect her own involvement in the mail ring. He needed to review the information the CID and MPs had accumulated thus far in case there was something he hadn't pieced together.

"Would you mind driving by Dani's quarters on the way to Kelly's?" Maggie glanced at her watch. "The photograph my neighbor sent should have arrived by now."

The tension in Maggie's face eased somewhat when Nate parked in front of Quarters 1448. Grateful for a momentary lull in the rain, they both stepped onto the sidewalk.

She pointed to the package sitting by the front door and brushed past him to retrieve the box. "Thank goodness the picture arrived in time."

Returning to the car with the package in hand, Maggie stopped short as a door opened across the street. The teenager with the piercings stepped onto his front porch. Seeing them, he turned and hurried back inside.

A military police sedan approached where Nate and Maggie stood. Sergeant Thorndike braked to a stop and leaned out the window. "Sir. Ma'am."

"Everything okay, Sergeant?"

Thorndike threw a glance at the now closed door of the quarters across the street. "Just keeping an eye on the hoodlum."

"The boy's name is Kyle Foglio, Sergeant. No matter how he looks, he's a family member living on post."

Clamping down on his jaw, the sergeant's face reddened with frustration. His brow wrinkled and crow's feet appeared at the corners of his eyes. Nate hadn't realized how the man had aged over the last few months. Thorndike was "short"—close to the twenty-year mark and ready to retire. He had told Nate on more than one occasion, he planned to buy a house on a lake in rural Florida and live the good life.

Nate had to wonder in the worsening economy if a military retirement would be adequate to sustain the sergeant and his family. Word was his wife had gotten into some credit card overspending trouble last year. Would the "little woman," as Thorndike called her, be happy living in the country far from the shopping malls she seemed to love?

"Did you get the message the provost marshal wanted to see you, sir?"

Nate nodded. "I'm scheduled to brief him at 1600 hours."

"Roger that."

The sergeant glanced once again at Lieutenant Colonel Foglio's quarters and rubbed his hand over his jaw as he turned back to Nate. "I did some investigating on my own, sir. Found out Mrs. Foglio took in the mail and watered the houseplants when Major Bennett was deployed and Graham Hughes was traveling due to his contract work."

Maggie inhaled sharply. "The family had a key to my sister's quarters?"

"That's right, ma'am."

Thorndike chewed on his lip, then narrowed his gaze as he looked first at the package Maggie still held in her hands and then at Nate. "The kid gave Agent McQueen a hard time, sir, so I'm not the only one who thinks he should be kicked off post."

The sergeant's voice was laced with attitude, which Nate chose to ignore. He'd give Thorndike the benefit of the doubt. Everyone had been working long hours and nerves were pulled thin, including his own.

"I'll see you at the briefing, Sergeant."

"Yes, sir." Thorndike touched his hand to his forehead in an informal salute and drove away.

Nate opened the passenger door for Maggie and after she was settled inside, he glanced, once again, at the quarters across the street. Kelly had brought Kyle Foglio in for questioning last summer after he had tried to buy beer on post using a false ID. The kid had gone berserk during the interrogation, shouting that she would pay for messing with a lieutenant colonel's son. Kelly had calmly instructed the father to control his child. To Lieutenant Colonel Foglio's credit, the boy had left post the following morning, supposedly because his mother wanted him back with her. No one had been sorry to see him go.

Was there a connection between Mrs. Foglio having a key to Quarters 1448 and Major Bennett's death? Seemed doubtful, yet Nate wouldn't disregard anything at this point. He wished he had more time to investigate. If only Chief Wilson, the head of Fort Rickman's CID unit, and the provost marshal on post weren't so set on classifying Major Bennett's death as a suicide.

Nate mulled over the information he had on the case as he drove in silence back to the BOQ. Before Maggie got out of the car, he reached for her hand. "Will you join me for dinner tonight?"

She nodded. "I'd like that. Can I run to the store and get anything? I saw a grocery just outside the main gate."

"You stay put at Kelly's. I'll throw something on the grill again so it'll be easy."

Nate felt a warm sense of anticipation as he drove back to headquarters despite the rain that started to fall with a vengeance. Then he thought about Major Bennett's funeral in the morning. Realizing tonight might be the last evening he'd have with Maggie, his optimism took a nosedive.

Somehow within the last forty-eight hours, Maggie Bennett had worked her way into— He sighed, knowing he might as well admit it. Maggie had worked her way into his heart.

After she left Fort Rickman and returned to Alabama, how long would it take him to get over her? Nate shook his head and groaned. Maybe a lifetime.

Maggie glanced at the clock in Kelly's kitchen and wondered when Nate would get home. Evidently the briefing had run long. Walking into the living area, she pulled back the curtains that covered the glassed upper portion of the back door and gazed at the sky. The last rays of the winter sun hung low on the horizon, and dark clouds were rolling in from the west, signaling more rain.

Earlier, a storm had caused additional problems for Freemont and the surrounding area. The evening news had mentioned growing concern as the river neared crest level in the downtown area. A local campground south of Freemont had been evacuated, and the townspeople were cautioned to stay clear of the raging water and the strong currents that threatened to wash everything downstream. At least Fort Rickman was on higher ground.

Maggie's cell phone chirped. She walked into the entryway where she'd left her purse on a small table by the door. Retrieving the phone, she glanced down at her sister's Bible, which she'd placed on the table earlier.

With her free hand, she touched the leather surface. The passage Dani had marked flashed through her mind.

Lord, how many times shall I forgive my brother when he sins against me? Dani had scratched out *brother* and inserted *sister* above the printed line.

Maggie shook her head ever so slightly. She didn't deserve forgiveness. Especially from her sister.

Knowing this wasn't the time to reflect on the meaning of the scripture or Dani's attempt to alter the text, Maggie raised the phone to her ear.

Kendra's panicked voice greeted her. "Someone broke into my house." Maggie gasped, but didn't get a chance to reply before Kendra continued. "Luckily I had taken my daughter to my mother's place to spend the night. When I returned, I saw the lock on the back door had been pried open. Whoever broke in, trashed my house. Papers were scattered everywhere."

"Did they take anything?"

"I can't find the CID agent's card. I had placed it on the windowsill above my sink in the kitchen, close to the phone. It's not there now, and it's not in the pile of rubble on the floor."

"Did you call the police?"

"I was too afraid. Someone might be watching my house. They could have seen Agent Patterson when you two talked to me yesterday." Kendra lowered her voice. "They're probably watching me still."

Maggie thought of the dark sedan that had followed her out of Kendra's neighborhood. "I'll call Nate. He'll come over to help you."

"No!" The woman's reply was sharp. "I don't want any more trouble. I called my mother and told her I was going out of town for a while. She'll take care of my baby girl."

"You can't run away."

"Isn't that what you and Dani did in high school?"

Maggie sighed. If only it had been that simple. "My father died. We were forced to move off post. My mother wanted to get away from this area. Besides, at the time you didn't seem to care much about what happened to Dani the way you literally left her holding the bag after the two of you were caught shoplifting."

"She told me that her dad would talk to the cops. That we'd both be okay. Instead she moved away, and I ended up getting caught anyway. I got a year in juvie."

"Dani didn't want to leave you or Freemont High."

"I don't know why she butted into my life in the first place." Anger replaced some of the fear Maggie had heard in Kendra's voice earlier. "For some reason, Dani wanted to be part of the gang, but she was from post. None of us had what she was used to."

"She needed a place to belong. That's what you gave her, Kendra."

"I don't know about that. I think my brother Rodney was the attraction. Someone said she used him to make Graham jealous. Then there was that rumor that he liked someone else. After you all moved, Graham changed, like he was hurt inside."

"Did he mention my sister?"

"He said someone had messed with his mind. He never mentioned anyone's name."

"That was high school, Kendra."

"Yeah, but things happen then and a person may never be able to move on. You know what I'm saying?"

Maggie did know, all too well.

"I saw Dani downtown in Freemont one day not too long after she moved back to Fort Rickman," Kendra continued. "She looked good dressed in her uniform. I was real proud of her, going into the service, like her dad. She used to tell me how much he loved her. I kept wondering what it would be like if my dad had stayed around. Sometimes I'd dream about having a father like you and Dani had, a father who loved me and doted on me."

Dani had painted a picture for Kendra that wasn't true. No matter how much Dani had craved attention, their father had turned a blind eye to her need to be loved. He'd turned a blind eye to Maggie, as well.

Nate's face played through her mind. Warmth washed over her. He represented what she had craved as a kid. Security. Affirmation. Someone who cared.

Kendra pulled in a ragged breath. "Listen, I've got to get out of here. Give me twenty-four hours. Then you can tell Agent Patterson, but if he steps in now, he'd do more harm than good."

"I don't like it, Kendra."

"But you owe me."

"For what?"

"For not telling Dani that you were the girl with Graham that night down at the river."

A warning pounded through Maggie's head and a roar filled her ears. Would that one mistake continue to dog her for the rest of her life? "Fine," she said. "Twenty-four hours. But Kendra, after that you've got to find a way to let me know you're all right. These people are dangerous. Don't trust anyone."

"Don't worry about me. I know how to take care of myself," Kendra replied. "I'll be fine."

Maggie froze, too shocked to even say goodbye as Kendra ended the call. *I'll be fine.* Those were the last words Dani had said to her two nights ago. Maggie wanted to believe that Kendra was going to be fine, that she had the situation under control, but she couldn't help but worry that, like Dani, Kendra's certainty that she'd be "fine" would turn out to be wrong. *Dead* wrong.

ELEVEN

Maggie stepped back into the kitchen and wrapped her arms around her waist, trying to focus on anything except Kendra's phone call. Nate. Dinner. Dani's funeral.

If only she had gone to the store as she had suggested to Nate earlier in the day. Surely he would be tired when he got home. She could have had dinner ready, if he hadn't insisted he had everything under control, which seemed to be his mantra.

Opening the refrigerator, she pulled out a head of lettuce, feeling confident Kelly wouldn't mind if she made a salad. Maggie found a bag of frozen peas and a heat-and-serve potato casserole in the freezer. Nate could grill the meat, but she would ensure the rest of the meal was prepared.

Cooking would occupy her hands and her mind and help to push aside everything Kendra had said. For the past two days, Maggie had focused on Dani and her funeral. Tonight Kendra had added another element that had Maggie worried. The element of danger. Would Kendra get hurt for answering the questions she and Nate had asked?

"Don't go there," she said aloud, forcing her mind

onto more pleasant thoughts like the way Nate had escorted her throughout the honor ceremony and how drop-dead gorgeous he looked in his uniform.

Drop-dead?

"Wrong choice of words," she mumbled as she washed the lettuce under a flow of cool water from the tap.

A sound startled her. She glanced into the living area at the glass portion of the rear door that opened onto a small back stoop.

Footsteps?

A tingle of concern played along her neck and put her nerve endings on alert.

There was no mistaking the sound. Someone was climbing the stairs to the back porch.

She turned off the water and sidled toward the refrigerator, hoping the nearby dividing wall to the rest of the apartment would block her from the view of anyone outside.

A lamp in the living area shone brightly, but the porch light was off, causing the window to reveal nothing except an expansive sea of black.

Again a shuffling sound came from outside. As Maggie watched, the doorknob turned. Her throat constricted. *Oh, no.*

The lock held, but seconds later, the sound of splintering wood filled her ears.

Where was the phone? She had to call for help.

She glanced furtively at her purse still sitting on the table in the entryway. Getting to her cell would place her in full view of the back door where the curtains hung open.

What about the landline? If only Kelly had an extension in the kitchen. Maggie flicked her eyes over the countertops then turned to gaze at the only noncellular phone she could see, which sat on an end table near the back door.

Another crack of wood sent slivers of fear ricocheting along her spine. Kendra had said someone had pried the lock off her door. Was the same person now trying to gain entry into Kelly's apartment?

Maggie glanced at the front door. Her car was in the parking lot. Would she be able to reach it in time? Or would the culprit round the apartment complex and grab her in the open lot? She needed her car keys, but they were in her purse. Could she move fast enough to escape?

Suddenly there was silence. Maggie strained to hear any noise that might indicate what would happen next. All she heard was the pounding of her heart.

She eased open the drawer where Kelly kept her silverware. Her fingers wrapped around a sturdy butcher knife, sharp enough to do damage, if she needed to defend herself.

Once again, she peered around the dividing wall.

Staring at the back door, she saw a shadowed form through the window. Lifting his arm, he hurled something at the—

A loud crash. Glass exploded.

Maggie screamed.

Run! an inner voice warned.

She dashed into the entryway. The back door creaked open, and glass crunched underfoot. Someone was inside the apartment, coming toward her.

A rush of adrenaline pushed her forward. She yanked her purse off the table and reached for the front doorknob, failing to unlatch the dead bolt. The knife dropped to the floor.

Using both hands, she flipped the bolt and turned the knob. The door flew open.

Cold, damp air swirled around her as she raced across the walkway. She spied her car, sitting in the parking area.

Movement. She glanced into the darkness, seeing someone in the shadows, barely able to sneak a glimpse as she ran as fast as she could.

Shaved head. A flash of metal. Body piercings?

Help me, Lord.

She fumbled with her purse as she ran. Where were her keys?

Footsteps sounded behind her.

She wouldn't make it to her car in time.

A hand grabbed her shoulder.

She jerked to get away.

"Maggie?"

The voice—

"Nate?" She turned, seeing his face twisted with concern. "Oh, thank God it's you."

She fell into his arms.

"What happened?" He pulled her back to stare into her eyes. "Tell me," he demanded.

She pointed to the BOQ. Her words came out in gasps. "Someone…someone tried…to break in. Glass shattered. The back door."

He grabbed her arm and encouraged her to move with him to where his car was parked. Opening the door, he handed her the keys. "Lock yourself in. If anyone approaches you, lay on the horn. I'll call for backup and check the rear of the complex."

He lifted his cell to his ear and punched in a number on speed dial. "This is Patterson. I'm at the BOQ complex. I need backup now."

After insuring she was safely locked inside his car, Nate raced toward the rear of the complex.

Maggie's heart hammered in her chest. She gasped for air. Dani was dead. Kendra was on the run.

And now Nate was heading right into the face of danger. She moaned, glancing once again to where Nate had disappeared around the corner of the large BOQ complex.

Not Nate. Please, dear Lord, keep him safe.

TWELVE

Nate found nothing behind the BOQ except broken glass and Kelly's back door hanging open. From the looks of the splintered wood, the perpetrator had tried to pry off the lock. When that hadn't worked, he had broken the glass in the window portion of the door. Careful not to disrupt evidence in the crime scene, Nate entered the apartment and checked to ensure the invader wasn't still inside.

The sound of sirens greeted Nate as he headed back to the parking lot. Maggie was sitting in his car, eyes wide and arms wrapped protectively around her shoulders. Two military police cars pulled into the lot and screeched to a stop.

"Dispatch said you had a problem, sir." Sergeant Thorndike saluted as he stepped from the sedan. Corporal Mills followed suit from the second car.

"Someone broke into Agent McQueen's BOQ. Apartment 2A. Shattered the glass on the back door." Nate glanced at Maggie. "Ms. Bennett was inside and ran out the front."

Nate pointed to the rear of the complex. "You men check out the back entrance. Dust for prints, and see what you can find while I talk to Ms. Bennett."

"Roger that, sir."

The two MPs double-timed around the corner and out of sight. Maggie released the lock and opened the car door as Nate approached.

"What did you find?" she asked.

"Shattered glass and an empty apartment."

"Did they take anything?"

"They? How many people did you see, Maggie?"

"A shadowed form at the back porch before the glass broke, but there was someone in the parking lot. He had a shaved head and was wearing jeans and a sweatshirt. I think it was the teen that lives across from Dani's house."

"You saw him?"

"Or someone who looked liked him."

"Let's get inside. Sergeant Thorndike and Corporal Mills are sweeping the back for evidence. I want you to check the apartment and ensure your things weren't disturbed."

Maggie went toward the bedrooms when they entered the apartment. Nate headed to the living area where the two MPs were working the crime scene. "Find anything?"

"Not yet, sir." Corporal Mills glanced up from dusting the door for prints. "Did Ms. Bennett get a visual?"

Nate shook his head. "Negative to the person who broke in."

"Would have made our job easier if she could ID someone," Thorndike said.

"But she did see a kid with a shaved head in the parking lot."

"Only one that comes to mind is Lieutenant Colonel Foglio's son." The sergeant turned to Mills. "Call it in.

See if one of our MPs can search the area. If the kid is still around, they'll find him."

Mills stepped outside to call as Maggie's footsteps sounded from the hallway. Approaching Nate, she said, "Nothing appears to have been disturbed in the bedrooms, but I found this on the floor." She held out a large shard of glass.

"I'll take that, ma'am." Thorndike stepped toward her and held open a plastic evidence bag into which she dropped the broken glass fragment.

"Probably stuck to the perpetrator's shoe." The sergeant looked at the bottom of his military boots. "See how they're imbedded in my soles?"

Maggie nodded then turned worried eyes to Nate. "That means he went into the guest bedroom."

"Evidently." Nate pointed around the living area. "Does anything appear to be moved around or missing?"

He followed Maggie's gaze as she looked at the photographs of Kelly and her mother, the books stacked on the coffee table, the teacup collection on a shelf in the corner.

She turned back to him and shook her head. "I don't notice anything out of place. Kelly's bedroom appeared neat and tidy, just the way she had left it."

Nate couldn't help but think of what would have happened to Maggie if he hadn't arrived home in time. He had checked his mailbox in the open-air walkway farther down the complex and was heading back to his BOQ when Kelly's door had opened and Maggie raced toward the parking lot. He'd run after her. When she'd turned to look into his eyes, he'd seen terror written across her face.

The Foglio teen had given Kelly problems last summer and had promised to make her pay. The kid needed to be brought in for questioning. If anything pointed to his involvement in the break-in, Nate would ensure he never stepped foot on Fort Rickman again.

"Sergeant Thorndike and Corporal Mills will handle everything here," Nate said to Maggie. "Let's go over to my place. I'll call Kelly and tell her what happened before I write up the report and fix you something to eat."

She shook her head. "I'm…I'm not hungry."

Her face was pale and reflected the shock she had to be feeling. Knowing she needed to get away from the scene of the crime, Nate placed his hand on the small of her back and ushered her toward the door. "I'll be back shortly," he told Thorndike.

Once inside his own apartment, Nate insisted Maggie relax while he contacted Kelly. She was relieved to know Maggie hadn't been hurt and promised to be back at Fort Rickman as soon as her investigation in North Georgia was over. After he hung up, Nate made a pot of coffee and fixed sandwiches for both of them. Nate filled out the paperwork electronically while Maggie sat on the couch and picked at her sandwich. Before he could submit the completed form, he glanced over, surprised as well as relieved to see she'd drifted to sleep.

Long lashes fanned her cheeks and a faint smile slipped over her full lips. *Please, Lord, allow her dreams to be as sweet as she is.*

Surprised by the thought, he tried to remember the last time he'd had any dialogue with the Lord. Certainly not since Michael's death. Maybe Maggie was rubbing off on him in a good way.

Nate had grown up in a strong Christian home, although his faith in God had never been more than lukewarm. After Michael's death, too many questions haunted Nate—questions about a loving God and the tragedy of a life cut short. Somehow the concept of a merciful Lord didn't work for a grief-stricken warrant officer who carried the blame for his younger brother's premature death.

Once again, a bad taste bubbled up from Nate's gut.

Was he making another mistake now? Despite his earlier prayer and the rising crime rate, he wasn't ready to buy into God nor was he totally convinced Dani had been murdered.

Quick as lightning, a vision of Maggie's body, lying in the pile of broken glass, flashed through his mind. Silken locks streamed around her lovely face as blood seeped from wounds made by a crazed intruder.

Nate's stomach roiled and a queasy sense of foreboding made him shiver. If Dani had been murdered, the killer could have come after Maggie tonight.

Maggie woke, hearing a door open. Her gaze flicked over the couch to the coffee table and the photo of Nate with his arm draped around his younger brother. Raking her fingers through her hair, she sat up, realizing she must have fallen asleep. Footsteps caused her to turn. Nate stood in the doorway.

"You're awake," he said, his voice upbeat.

"Sorry, I dozed off."

"I doubt you've gotten much sleep these last few nights." He walked to where she sat. "They boarded up the broken window with plywood and cleaned up the glass. It's a temporary fix, but you'll be safe tonight."

"Did you learn anything new about what happened?"

"We pulled in Lieutenant Colonel Foglio's son for questioning. He admitted walking across the parking lot to get to his girlfriend's house. She lives in the next housing area. The dad confirmed the kid's story."

Maggie heard hesitation in his voice. "But?"

"But there's a more direct path so he must have planned his route to include the detour. Kelly came down hard on Kyle last summer when he first appeared on our radar. The kid claimed he'd make her pay."

"Where's Kyle now?"

"Being held overnight. I told his dad the experience might make him realize where he's headed, if he doesn't do an about-face."

"Did the dad agree?"

Nate nodded. "He knows if his son is involved in a crime, the commanding general will be notified. Foglio could be relieved of his position on post and transferred to another duty station because of his son. He used to oversee the contractors on post and had to travel a lot. Now he's got a better job he wouldn't want to lose."

Maggie shook her head, feeling a swell of anger and frustration. "That's the army way, isn't it? If there's a problem with a kid, you ship off the family to another installation." A jumble of memories played through her mind of the MPs talking to her parents, mention of the chain of command, her father being called in to see the commanding general.

Nate furrowed his brow. "You know a soldier who has kids—whether he's an officer or a noncommissioned officer or enlisted—has to be responsible for his family members' actions on post, Maggie. If a man can't control an unruly teen, how is he going to handle a company or battalion or brigade of men during combat?"

"It all comes down to the mission, doesn't it, Nate? Combat. War fighting."

"We don't focus on war, Maggie. Ask any soldier, and he or she will tell you that we're peacekeepers first. Sometimes the only way to ensure the peace is to stand up for what is right."

"And what about you, Nate? Are you keeping the peace, or trying to find my sister's killer? I told you, Graham killed her."

"How can you be so sure?"

Needing to convince Nate of Graham's guilt, she said, "Dani and Graham dated for a while during high school. When their relationship started to got bad, she tried to make him jealous by flirting with other guys. A rumor circulated that Graham was interested in someone else. Then there was a party down by the river with no adult supervision." She shrugged. "You know kids."

Nate nodded.

"Dani and Graham broke up, and a few days later, I heard our dog barking. Spike was a good watchdog, but he was chained in the backyard and couldn't defend himself. By the time I got outside, Graham had slit his throat." Remembering the dying animal's gasps for air brought tears to Maggie's eyes.

"And your dad, Maggie?"

"He died soon thereafter."

Nate let out a lungful of pent-up air.

"Last night someone called Kelly's landline." Maggie swiped at the wayward tear that escaped down her cheek.

"The first time, I thought it was a prank call. The second time he whispered Spike's name." She glanced up at Nate. "It had to have been Graham."

Nate's eyes narrowed. "Why didn't you tell me earlier?"

"I…I didn't think you'd understand."

He sighed with frustration. "What else did the caller say?"

"Nothing else."

"But you think it was Graham because he mentioned your dog's name? Did you see Graham kill your dog?"

She raised her hands. "Why do you always doubt what I tell you?"

"Did anyone see Graham do it?" Nate pressed.

"No, but I heard him gloating at school over how upset Dani was about it. He all but admitted he'd done it. But you're missing the point. If the caller last night wasn't Graham, how would he know about Spike?"

Nate shook his head as if she were making up the story. Why didn't he believe her? "You don't bend, do you, Nate?"

He raised his brow. "Bend?"

"It's your way or no way. Aren't I right? Was that what happened in Afghanistan with your brother? Did you boys get into an argument so you lashed out at him? He got hot under the collar, hurled a few negative comments your way and then stomped off and got himself killed?"

The muscles in Nate's neck stiffened. She had said something that hit too close to the truth he always demanded from her.

The phone rang. In that split second, he slipped back

into agent mode. He glanced at the caller ID and lifted the cell to his ear. "Patterson."

His face darkened, his eyes lowered. "Do you have a positive ID?" He nodded in response to something the caller said. "That's right. A young daughter."

Maggie's stomach tightened.

"Have you notified the grandmother?" Nate paused, listening. "Roger that. Let me know any further developments." He slipped his cell back into his pocket before he looked at Maggie.

"It's Kendra, isn't it?" she asked.

Nate pulled in a breath before he spoke. "The Freemont police IDed a body they pulled from the river. The name they have is Kendra Adams."

"Oh, no." Maggie's hand flew to her mouth.

"The police found her car on the side of the road near a bend in the river. Evidently, she was trying to leave town. Suitcases were in the back of her car. She told her mother she would return for her daughter as soon as she could."

"Why did she park close to the river? The news reports have been warning people about the strong current."

"She'd been forced from her car, Maggie. Her arms were scraped, and there were marks around her neck. Kendra had been dragged to the river's edge and strangled to death before her body ever entered the water."

Maggie's chest constricted. She shook her head, unable to accept the senselessness of another death. "Ken…Kendra called me earlier and said someone had tried to break into her house. Whoever it was pried the lock off her back door."

"You should have told me. I could have notified the police. They would have increased surveillance."

"She said the police would cause her more trouble and begged me to keep silent for twenty-four hours. They were watching her, weren't they, Nate?"

"More than likely. They must have known she had talked to us."

"There was a dark sedan that followed me out of Kendra's neighborhood and all the way to the pawnshop."

Nate nodded. "I saw it, too."

"But you didn't mention it?"

"I didn't want to worry you."

"The person or persons who killed Kendra could be the same people who killed Dani."

"I still don't have anything to substantiate that theory. Jamison questioned Graham again this afternoon."

"Did he make up another alibi?"

"He was with Wanda."

"And you believe him?"

"Maggie, it's not just me. The head of the CID unit here at Rickman, Chief Agent-in-Charge Wilson is convinced your sister's death was a suicide."

"What about the smuggling operation and Kendra's murder?"

"We're not even sure what Dani uncovered in Afghanistan. Show me evidence, Maggie. I need something to prove a tie-in."

"What about the list of names and post office boxes?"

"That's not enough to hold up in court."

"I thought military justice didn't need evidence." She huffed.

"Oh, come on. You're being unreasonable. Evidence

is needed in a military court of law just as it is in a civilian court."

"Some of my things were out of place when I opened my suitcase at Kelly's apartment. Did you have a soldier rifle through my suitcase without a search warrant the night Dani died."

"He took the initiative on his own, Maggie, which was the wrong thing to do. I talked to him about it later, but as you recall, we were investigating a possible homicide."

"So you're admitting Dani was murdered?"

"I'm saying initially murder couldn't be ruled out."

"And now?"

"Now, I'm not sure."

"You're blinded to the truth, Nate."

"Why is it so hard for you to believe your sister took her own life just as your father did?" He stared at her for a moment. "It's you, isn't it? You feel responsible for both of their deaths."

His words stung as if he'd slapped her with his hand. Digging her fingernails into her palms, she steeled herself, unwilling to let him see the effect his accusation had on her.

Lowering her voice, she spoke slowly and distinctly. "You're the one who struggles with responsibility issues, Nate. What did you do that makes you feel the blame for your brother's death?"

Once again, he stared at her as if weighing whether to divulge the secrets he carried. "Okay." He nodded. "I'll tell you the truth. Then maybe you'll share your story with me."

Suddenly, she wasn't sure she wanted him to continue.

He lowered himself onto the couch and put his head in his hands for a long minute. When he finally looked up, his face was stretched tight. "I'd gotten word Michael's best friend had made some black market sales to the Afghanis. It's a problem over there. Cigarettes are a big ticket item. The evidence was shaky, and my brother went to bat for the guy. Said he was a good soldier and did everything by the book."

The pulse throbbed on Nate's neck. "I should have gone with my initial gut reaction, but because Michael vouched for the guy, I gave him a pass. But when new evidence came in against him, I couldn't ignore it. I had no choice but to bring him in for questioning. Michael thought I was shoving my weight around because I didn't like the guy and that I'd been out to get him from the start."

Nate ran his hands over his face. Maggie knew the next part of the story would be more difficult to tell.

"My brother had come back from patrol a few hours earlier and hadn't caught any shut-eye. Unbeknownst to me, he was tasked to pull his friend's patrol duty—the duty the guy couldn't do because I had him in custody."

A lump formed in Maggie's throat. The ending was one she didn't want to hear, but she couldn't stop Nate now.

He looked at her with somber eyes that revealed the pain he carried. "The last time I saw Michael, he was heading out of the forward operating base, lead Humvee in the convoy. The only thing he said to me was 'Thanks a lot.'"

She scooted closer and rubbed her fingers over his arm. "Oh, Nate, I'm so sorry."

"Had I hauled the guy in when I first suspected wrong doing, he might have confessed, and my brother would still be alive."

"You're not responsible."

"None of this would have happened if I had done my job and questioned the guy until he told the truth." Nate's crystal-blue eyes turned on her.

Suddenly, the focus was on Maggie. "Do...do you still think I'm not telling the truth?"

"You didn't tell me about the prank caller last night, Maggie, or about Kendra leaving Freemont. I think you're keeping something else from me. Something about what happened long ago. It all ties together, doesn't it? Your father's death, Dani going into the military."

Maggie felt exposed. Nate knew she was to blame. She could see it in the way his brow furrowed and his gaze narrowed. No matter what, she could never tell him what had started the terrible chain reaction that led to her father's death. She'd rather turn her back on him now, than open a wound she had tried so hard to heal.

"I need to lie down, Nate. I'll keep my cell on and call you if I have a problem."

Rising from the couch, she hurried to the door. He raced after her and grabbed her arm. "Are you running away?"

She hesitated. "I...I guess I am. Just like you've been running away, Nate. You can't help me until you get over your brother's death." She searched his face. "What I don't understand is that you have a family. You could tell them what happened. They'll know you're not to blame."

Because they love you, she failed to add as she ran from his BOQ and locked herself in Kelly's apartment.

Maggie needed to distance herself from Nate's penetrating gaze that went straight to her core and saw the essence of who she truly was. Did he realize she didn't deserve to be loved? She had caused too much pain, too much death.

Everything started long ago with a terrible mistake she had made, never realizing the effect it would have on too many people's lives.

But now she was back in the place where it had all fallen apart, and the last of her family was dead. Could she bear to stay and find answers, to prove the guilt of her sister's killer, or would her own guilt drive her away again?

THIRTEEN

As much as Nate wanted to race after Maggie, he had to let her go. She was running away from something in her past, just as Nate had tried to escape the reality of Michael's death. Maggie was right. Nate had turned his back on his family, not the other way around. Maybe they deserved to know what had led up to Michael being on patrol that fateful day, but Nate wasn't ready to expose himself to more pain.

He glanced at his watch. Mentally adjusting to the time in Afghanistan, he retrieved a number from the contact list on his cell and hit the call key, relieved when a voice answered on the other end.

"This is Mr. Patterson, CID, Fort Rickman, Georgia. I called yesterday and spoke to Special Agent Damian Jones. Is he available?"

"Yes, sir. I'll get him for you."

Nate drummed his fingers on his desk until the agent came on the line. "Unfortunately, I don't have answers for you yet," Damian said in greeting. "We brought in the dogs and searched the area, looking for earthenware figurines as well as drugs. Nothing turned up. Funny, though. After your phone call yesterday, I kept think-ing about the improvised explosive device that killed

Captain York and the other soldier in the 2nd Transport. It had been bothering me before, but after talking to you, I decided we needed to give it a relook. My people are combing through the wreckage yet again. No one's happy, but, I promise you, if there's anything that points to U.S. soldiers setting the IED, we'll find it."

"Something concerned you about the way the explosive had been rigged?" Nate checked the file he had opened on his computer and paused for a long moment as his words traveled halfway around the world. "Your exact words were 'the device looked too sophisticated.'"

"That's right. Not that the local terrorists don't copycat everything we do, but this was a perfect replica and screamed *Made in the USA*." Damian let out a deep sigh. "Hard enough when the enemy strikes. Having someone on our side involved decimates morale, yet we both know there are evil men who would do anything for their own gain."

"Even kill."

"Roger that. I'll contact you if anything turns up."

Nate disconnected, thinking of what Damian had said about copycats and perfect replicas. Had Dani's death been an exact copy of her father's suicide? Scrolling through the archived CID files, Nate pulled up the report on Lieutenant Colonel Bennett's death sixteen years ago. As Jamison had mentioned, the information was sketchy, either because the person who had updated the database failed to include all the details or because the actual hardcopy report had been less than complete.

Another search revealed a Colonel Glen Rogers, who had been the provost marshal at that time, commanding the military police on post. Hopefully he would remember the death investigation his MPs had conducted.

Knowing military personnel often retire at their last duty station and remain in the local area, Nate flipped through the pages of the Freemont phone directory and quickly found a listing for Glen Rogers, Colonel Retired. He plugged the number into his cell but was routed to voice mail. Nate left a brief message and asked the colonel to contact him at his first convenience.

Needing to clear the cobwebs that clogged his brain and wanting to ensure Maggie was safe, Nate pulled a fleece jacket from his closet and left his apartment. The bright lighting in the open walkway outside provided a good deterrent to keep perpetrators from approaching the front of the complex. The rear, on the other hand, sat cloaked in darkness and backed onto a wooded area, where Nate now headed.

Earlier while Maggie had catnapped, he'd tested the plywood Thorndike and Mills had used to shore up Kelly's broken window. The makeshift fix secured the rear entrance, but Nate needed to confirm no one was hanging around in the shadows. Rounding the complex, he moved quietly into a stand of trees where he had a clear view of the entire area.

His eyes quickly acclimated to the dark, and he scanned the shrubbery and underbrush but saw nothing suspicious. The crickets and cicadas chirped their night songs accompanied by an occasional tree frog while a light mist added more moisture to the damp and chilly night.

Lights blazed inside Kelly's BOQ, and Nate imagined Maggie curled up on the couch, arms wrapped protectively around her waist. Although Nate wanted to provide the protection she needed, he had to give her the freedom she demanded.

When the first morning light filtered over the horizon, Nate left the woods and headed back to his BOQ for a quick shower and a pot of high-test coffee. He downed three cups while rehashing his conversation with Damian Jones. *Copycat* kept circulating through his mind.

On his way to the kitchen to pour a fourth cup, his cell rang. "Patterson."

"Corporal Otis, sir. That toxicology report you wanted arrived." Nate listened to the results then disconnected and pushed speed dial for Kelly's cell. Her voice sounded groggy when it came over the line.

"I need to bounce some ideas around, concerning Major Bennett's death. Do you mind?"

She groaned. "At this time of night?"

"The sun's up, Kel. It's morning."

"Not in North Georgia. Besides, you're entirely too energetic."

"Sorry, but it's important. I keep thinking about the attic light being off when Maggie found her sister. Seems to me if Major Bennett killed herself, she wouldn't turn off the light. Plus, her shoes were downstairs under a table."

"Hmm?" Kelly had taken the bait and now seemed interested in reviewing the case. "Maybe she had a few obsessive-compulsive tendencies and liked everything nice and neat."

"Yes, but it's winter. Those old quarters are drafty, yet she climbed the stairs to the attic without shoes."

"And you're saying what?"

Nate wasn't sure what he was trying to establish, but voicing the problem out loud sometimes helped the pieces fall into place. "Let's consider what would happen if someone had killed her and then tried to make it look like suicide. There were no visible signs of a struggle. What's that tell you?"

"That she had been incapacitated in some way. Probably drugged."

"Maybe the perpetrator slipped something into her wineglass, which he wiped clean and placed on a rack in the dishwasher."

Kelly played along. "Her shoes could have fallen off as he carried her up the stairs."

"Exactly. Later he would have wiped them, as well, and then placed them under a table."

"If prints had been removed, the person understood how cops gather evidence."

"And who would best know those procedures, Kelly?"

"Another cop?"

"Bingo."

"Ah, Nate." Kelly sighed. "You could be getting into hot water with this one."

"But the pieces fit, *if* she were murdered. The shoes, the two wineglasses. Plus, Maggie said the attic was dark when she found her sister. No reason for the major to turn off the light before she put the noose around her neck. But someone leaving the attic might pull the light switch, knowing a dark house with a lone light shining through the attic dormer window would draw suspicion."

"He—or she—never expected Maggie to show up that night," Kelly added.

"That's right. Had Major Bennett been found in the daytime, the light may not have been noticed."

"What about the tox screen?" Kelly asked.

"I just got the report. Her specimen was positive for

benzodiazepines. Specifically alprazolam. You might know it by the trade name Xanax. Interestingly, a civilian doctor prescribed Xanax for Major Bennett the week prior to her death."

"She could have popped a few pills to overcome any last-minute anxiety if she were planning to take her own life."

Kelly's comment held water, yet the major seemed like a woman who stood by her decisions. If she had decided to commit suicide, she wouldn't turn to chemical aids to get her through it.

"She kept her pills in a kitchen cabinet," Nate added. "The killer could have used her own prescription meds to drug her."

"Did you get the results for the residue left in the wineglass on the counter?" Kelly asked.

"Negative for Xanax, and the glass in the dishwasher had been wiped clean."

"Had the perpetrator planned to kill her from the get-go?"

"I'm not sure, Kel. But suppose someone in law enforcement stopped by her house to talk to her. The major told her sister that she had uncovered something unsettling in Afghanistan and suspected law enforcement could be involved."

"You're saying Major Bennett trusted the killer and invited him into her house to discuss the situation."

"That's it exactly. Only, he's in on the deal and realizes she needs to be silenced. She may have left the pills on the counter. If she stepped out of the kitchen for a minute or two, he would have had enough time to slip the drugs into her glass."

"Wouldn't she recognize the medicinal taste?"

"Maggie told me that her sister didn't like red wine—she might not have been familiar enough with the taste to suspect anything."

"Yet she drank it that night?"

Nate sighed. "Work with me, Kelly. Maybe the cop convinced her wine would help her relax."

"Only, the combination of drugs and alcohol knocked her out. He carried her upstairs and made her death look like it was self-inflicted."

"And identical to the way her father died sixteen years earlier."

"Time out, Nate. How does the guy know about the dad's death?"

"Good question." And one Nate couldn't answer. Unless…? The killer had to have known the family and understood the importance of Major Bennett following in her father's footsteps. Graham had an alibi, but things weren't always as they seemed.

Nate's neck tingled. Maybe Maggie had been right about Graham all along.

FOURTEEN

The next morning, Maggie woke with a dull ache in her temples and a stiff spine. She'd fallen asleep on the couch in Kelly's living area, close enough to the plywood-covered back door to hear any shuffling sounds outside should the assailant try to gain entry again. Cell phone in hand, she'd been ready to contact Nate at the first indication of anything suspicious. The last time she had checked the time, the clock in the kitchen had read 4:00 a.m.

Maggie made a pot of coffee, but the hot brew stuck in her throat, and she ended up pouring it down the drain. Once dressed, she waited for Nate who looked equally out of sorts when she opened the door to his knock. At other times, his presence had buoyed her flagging spirits, but today the memory of the way they had parted last night added to the melancholy day.

They rode in relative silence to the Main Post Chapel where the hearse sat in the driveway. Maggie steeled herself to what lay ahead before she walked into the chapel where Dani's casket waited in the narthex. The honor guard took their positions on either side of the casket as the first strains of organ music filtered through the church. A sea of mourners filled the sanctuary and turned to watch Maggie's slow procession down the center aisle behind the casket to her seat in the front pew on the left.

Graham sat across from her on the opposite side of the aisle, looking tired. Dark circles rimmed his eyes, due, no doubt, to late nights spent with the woman from the bar and grill. The thought of him racing into the arms of another woman the night Dani had died filled Maggie's stomach with bile. She wanted to walk across the aisle and slap his face. Instead, she tugged at the edge of her jacket and kept her eyes facing forward, unwilling to acknowledge his presence.

Someone had placed the photographs of her sister and family on a small table near the altar along with a bud vase containing one yellow rose. Maggie stared at the pictures, trying to find something good on which to focus. At this moment, all she could think about was the senseless waste of life.

Nate slipped into the pew next to her. As much as she appreciated his support, she felt betrayed by his inability to realize what had really happened that fateful night. Was he still so hung up on his own brother's death that he was unable to make an accurate judgment about her sister's murder?

The funeral passed in a blur. The all-male choir of uniformed soldiers sang patriotic hymns that dated back to Civil War days. After the last strains of an especially moving selection ended, an officer in Dani's unit read from scripture about the many mansions the Lord had prepared for those who died.

Similar words had been intoned at her father's funeral, but Maggie had been too young to realize the long-term consequences of that death. Once again, her throat thickened and tears streamed down her cheeks. She wiped them with a tissue and gritted her teeth, determined not to let Nate or Graham have the satisfaction of seeing her pain.

Chaplain Grant moved to the pulpit. Maggie focused on the scripture he read and the kind words he said about Dani and her career in the army. He exalted her heroism and love of country, and his praise brought a lump of pride to Maggie's throat and more tears to her eyes.

At the conclusion of the service, the pallbearers took their places beside the casket and, with uniform precision, began their return march to the hearse. Maggie walked behind the honor guard. Once the casket had been placed within the waiting vehicle, Nate took her arm and ushered her to the limousine provided by the funeral home.

She settled into the rear seat. Nate climbed in beside her, sitting close enough for Maggie to feel the heat from his body. Although aware of his nearness, she kept her eyes trained on the passing landscape and clamped her jaw together, trying to keep the tears at bay.

The graveside service passed in another wave of readings from scripture, punctuated with a rifle salute in honor of Dani's service and concluded with a lone bugler and the doleful twenty-six notes of Taps that echoed over the hallowed ground.

Twice during the short ride back to the church, Nate tried to draw her into conversation, but both times, Maggie held up her hand and shook her head. She wasn't ready to discuss anything except how much she regretted her sister's death. He reached for her arm when he helped her from the car, but she moved out of his grasp, knowing any act of kindness would unleash the tide of tears she was trying so hard to contain.

The well-wishers seemed sincere at the reception where food lined a huge table not far from where she stood. A mix of civilians and military in uniform formed an impromptu receiving line to offer their condolences. After they expressed words of sympathy, they filled their plates with food and chatted amicably with others who gathered in small clusters around the fellowship hall.

The heartfelt sympathy of the people at Fort Rickman warmed Maggie's heart. Their comments reflected their honest admiration for Dani. The positive impact she had had on so many lives was in direct contrast to the dark mood that had been so present at their father's funeral.

Encouraged by the support for her sister, Maggie realized she had been too hard on Nate. If he were like the other military officers and noncommissioned officers she had met today, he only wanted to serve his country and do the best job possible.

Nate brought her a glass of water, which he placed on a side table near where she stood. She appreciated the gesture and recalled their first encounter, when the same small token of his concern had struck a warm chord in her grief-stricken heart. Could it only have been less than seventy-two hours since they'd met?

As the line of mourners dwindled at last, she looked around the hall, searching for Nate. He was standing by his commander, Chief Warrant Officer and Agent-in-Charge Wilson, a tall African-American who Maggie had met immediately after the service. As much as she had wanted to talk to the chief, she refused to discuss the sensitive subject of her sister's death with so many people standing nearby.

Better to approach Chief Wilson now. Nate knew the way she felt and had heard her arguments before. Maybe he would even lend support. Relieved to finally have an opportunity to state her case to the CID commander, and with the funeral behind her, Maggie felt her spirits lift. As she neared the two men, the words she overheard Chief Wilson utter made her euphoria plummet into despair.

"I signed your request for transfer to the 105th Airborne." Chief Wilson patted Nate's shoulder. "Hate to see you leave us here at Fort Rickman to head back to Afghanistan, but I understand your desire to rejoin the fight as soon as possible. The unit's due to deploy in three weeks. If I place a rush on the request, you should be able to join them within a fortnight. I just need to know if you can be ready to leave post that soon."

Maggie tried to breathe. Nate was leaving Fort Rickman and returning to Afghanistan?

"I'll get back to you on that, sir." Nate turned from his commander and caught sight of her. His face opened into a smile. Did he realize she'd overheard his plans to leave Rickman and, in so doing, leave her, as well?

"Corporal Mills drove your car over from the BOQ and parked it in the church lot," Nate said, oblivious to the effect the information was having on Maggie. He dug in his pocket for the keys to her car and handed them to her. "I won't be able to give you a ride back since one of the Postal Inspectors called me a few minutes ago."

She tried to focus on the words he was saying, but she couldn't get around the fact that in just a few weeks, he was scheduled to deploy—a deployment Nate had requested.

"A package mailed from an APO in Afghanistan arrived at the Garrett post office," he continued. "The inspector hopes they'll be able to detain the point of contact when he moves in to claim the box. I need to be on-site. Things should move along quickly, and I plan to be back on post by late-afternoon."

Nate was sidestepping the issue of his deployment and letting her believe he was still determined to find what Dani had uncovered in Afghanistan.

"Maybe we can go out for dinner tonight?" His eyes held no hint of guile as he stared at her.

"Maybe. Give me a call when you get back." Hopefully, he couldn't see the pain she tried to mask. "Excuse me for a minute."

Turning her back to him, she headed toward the ladies' room. Her head pounded, and the tears that had threatened to spill returned once again. Nate had known all along he was leaving post.

Don't rock the boat. Was that it?

He didn't want to do anything to counter his boss or infringe on Chief Wilson's agreement to accept Nate's request for transfer. No wonder he hadn't investigated Dani's death further.

"Maggie?"

She turned at the sound of Chaplain Grant's voice. He followed her into the hallway. "I would be happy to drive you back to your lodging. I know this is a difficult day."

She scrubbed her hand over her face, attempting to wipe away her seemingly perpetual trail of tears. "My car is parked outside, Chaplain, so I'll be able to drive myself back to Agent McQueen's BOQ, but thank you for the kind words you said about my sister today."

"All true." He looked at her with compassion, causing her determination to hold her tears at bay to falter and nearly crumble into oblivion. She tried to smile, but didn't succeed, and knew her dam of self-control would soon break if she didn't get away.

"If you'll excuse me," she said in parting. "I need to freshen my makeup." Instead of the ladies' restroom, she headed for the side door and quickly made her way outside.

Packing the few things she had at Kelly's BOQ wouldn't take long and then she would head back to Alabama, much as she regretted the way she was leaving post. Her sister's murder hadn't been resolved, but Maggie couldn't remain at Fort Rickman any longer.

At some point in the last seventy-two hours, she had started to believe everything would end differently. In fact, she'd even thought that something ongoing could continue with Nate. Now she knew he wasn't interested in making their relationship more lasting.

"Good riddance," she grumbled. Then she thought about his warm gaze and the way her heart fluttered whenever he was near. The realization of her true feelings shook her to the core. Despite everything that had happened and even though he was leaving her behind, Maggie had to admit the truth. She had fallen in love with Nate Patterson.

Nate watched Maggie head to the ladies' room. All morning, she had been quiet and withdrawn as he had expected she would be during her sister's funeral. Silly to think Maggie would have been affected by the magnetism that had drawn him to her right from the start. She had closed all doors to her inner world and hung a "Do Not Disturb" sign on her heart. Would this evening be different or would she still be hiding behind the permanent divider she refused to tear down?

Someone tapped his shoulder. Nate turned to see an older gentleman, probably early seventies, who held out his hand. "Mr. Patterson, my name is Glen Rogers."

The provost marshal at Fort Rickman when Maggie's father had died. Nate shook his hand. "Nice to meet you, sir."

"I've been out of town, visiting my daughter and grandchildren and drove back in time for the service today. I found your voice mail on my phone but didn't have an opportunity to call you prior to the funeral. You wanted information?"

"That's correct." Classrooms surrounded the main fellowship hall, and Nate motioned the retired colonel into the closest empty space and shut the door behind them. "We should be able to talk privately in here, sir."

"Your message mentioned Dan Bennett's death."

"Yes, sir. The case file was rather sketchy. I'm investigating his daughter Major Bennett's death, and the circumstances are similar."

"From what I've heard, she copied her father in many ways." The retired colonel shook his head. "Such a shame."

"Do you recall any information about the circumstances of the lieutenant colonel's suicide? Anything that might have bearing on the daughter's death."

"How could I forget? Dan's wife had cancer and needed a costly treatment the army refused to cover. He was the head of comptroller's shop on post at that time, which, as you know, handles funding. Dan uncovered two noncommissioned officers who were altering the books for their own gain."

"Embezzling money from Uncle Sam?"

"Regrettably, yes. Dan was worried about his wife, so he took a bribe to remain quiet and to help pay for the treatment she needed. At least that's what he confessed when one of the NCO's pilfering came to light. In deference to Dan's long career and because of the situation, the commanding general accepted his resignation in return for exposing the second man in the operation. Dan planned to retire quietly. Major General Able, the post CG, ordered me to wipe the record clean of Dan's involvement."

"But he took his own life before he could retire?"

"Dan feared he'd have to testify in court. He didn't want his daughters to find out about his wrongdoing. He was a reserved man who took his job seriously. Unfortunately, he had made a bad decision that he couldn't live with. Of course, his daughters had gotten into trouble just a few days earlier. Dani had been picked up for shoplifting by the Freemont police."

"You were notified?"

"That's right. Major Bennett gave her parents fits. She'd started to run with a rather wild group of local town kids."

"Do you know anything about a pet being killed?"

The retired colonel nodded, his eyes solemn. "The second NCO, whose name hadn't been revealed at that time, killed the dog to warn Dan to keep his mouth shut."

"So none of the kids from high school were involved in the dog's death?"

"That's right, but losing the pet made Dan realize he needed to come clean. In return, we attempted to keep his involvement closely held. Only a handful of people on post knew what had really happened. The commanding general and his aide, as well as a few people in the JAG office who were working on the embezzlement case."

"Were there suspicions the Lieutenant Colonel's death was anything except a suicide?"

"None whatsoever. He hung himself late one night from a rafter in his home."

"Do you recall if the light was left on in the attic?"

"I may be getting old, Mr. Patterson, but my memory's sharp. The attic light alerted one of my men on patrol. The CG was big on energy conservation and had ordered all unnecessary lights to be turned off at night. An MP on duty stopped by the house, despite the late hour. Mrs. Bennett went to the attic and found her husband."

Nate could only imagine her shock.

"Fact is," the colonel continued, "I ran into that soldier not long ago in the Post Exchange. He's back at Fort Rickman and ready to retire. You probably know Sergeant Thorndike."

A thread of concern tangled up Nate's spine. Thorndike had never mentioned knowing about Lieutenant Colonel Bennett's death. "Sir, you said the *daughters* had been in trouble, but you only mentioned the shoplifting incident. Had the younger sister been involved, as well?"

The colonel rubbed his hand over his jaw and thought

for a moment. "A party down by the river as I recall. The Freemont police busted up the gathering and drove everyone home. Dan's younger daughter was part of the group so I was notified."

"Both girls had run-ins with the law shortly before their father's death?"

"That's why I told Mrs. Bennett they needed to know the truth about their father. Teens are totally absorbed in their own worlds. I feared the girls would think their father had taken his life because of what they had done. That's a lot of guilt for any young person to carry."

"Yes, sir. Regrettably, that guilt could follow them into adulthood." After thanking the colonel for his help, Nate returned to the fellowship hall.

The crowd had dispersed and only a few people remained. The women who had prepared the luncheon were cleaning up the serving table. Chaplain Grant stood nearby, fork in hand.

"Glad you finally had time to eat, sir." Nate noticed as assortment of desserts piled high on his plate.

"Not what the doctor ordered since I should be cutting calories, but I couldn't resist."

Glancing around the hall, Nate asked, "Have you seen Maggie?"

The chaplain pointed toward the hallway. "She was headed for the ladies' room about thirty minutes ago. I haven't seen her since."

With a hasty word of thanks, Nate hurried outside. The parking lot had emptied. Not a silver Saturn in sight.

His phone rang. He checked the caller ID as he pulled the cell to his ear. "Hey, Jamison. What's up?"

"A guy has been hanging around outside the post

office in Garrett. The inspectors think it may be Lance Davis, who was the contact name for this P.O. on the list we found in Major Bennett's quarters. They're ready to close in. You need to get here ASAP."

"Is Sergeant Thorndike with you?"

"I expect him in the next ten minutes or so."

"Don't let him leave the area."

Nate double-timed to his car. He had some important questions to ask Thorndike about why he hadn't been forthright about the late Lieutenant Colonel Bennett's death. With any luck, the sergeant might provide more details about the initial suicide, which could have bearing on Major Bennett's death.

Pulling onto the main road that headed off post, Nate thought about calling Maggie, but the new information he had learned about her father needed to be revealed in person.

He and Maggie had more in common than he had ever realized. They both felt responsible for the loss of a loved one. Maggie had tried to help him move beyond the guilt he still carried because of Michael. Even if Nate couldn't clear his own conscience, he wanted to help Maggie get over her father's death. Bottom line, she wasn't to blame. But after sixteen years of feeling responsible, Maggie would need time to accept the truth about what had happened so long ago.

FIFTEEN

After changing into the orange sweater and jeans she had worn on the drive to Fort Rickman, Maggie packed her bag and threw it into the back of her Saturn. She wrote a note of thanks to Kelly and then headed out of the BOQ complex. Thoughts of her father rumbled through her mind. She needed something of his to hold on to, something that would remind her of the man she loved whether he had loved her or not.

The front entrance into the Hunter Housing Area was blocked by a utility truck parked in the middle of the road while a man worked on the streetlight. A detour sign routed her into the alley that ran behind the quarters. Maggie entered her sister's house through the back door and headed straight to the coffee table in the living room.

Just as Dani had done, Maggie would display the flag, which had draped their father's casket, and the shadowbox that contained his medals in her own home. If Graham would part with her sister's medals, Maggie would sit them alongside their father's awards. When people asked, she'd say Dani had followed in his footsteps and both had died while serving their country.

Maggie found a plastic bag in the kitchen pantry.

After wrapping the chosen items in newsprint, she carefully placed them in the bag then stopped short when the garage door rumbled open.

Her heart pattered in her chest. "Nate?"

An MP stepped into the kitchen. She recognized him as Corporal Mills—the soldier who had no doubt searched her bag the night of Dani's death. "I saw your car and wondered what you were doing here, ma'am."

Before she could answer, the doorbell rang. "I'll get it." Maggie scurried into the foyer, wishing Nate would be waiting on the doorstep. Instead she saw a teenage boy, heavily tattooed with a silver stud in his left nostril.

"My stepmom said the mailman delivered this to the wrong address." The teen shoved a package into Maggie's hands before he ran back across the street. The address label had been written in Dani's hand.

A sense of relief and elation swept over Maggie. At long last, she had evidence that, hopefully, would prove her sister had been murdered.

Closing the door, Maggie turned, surprised to discover the MP blocking her way.

"I'll take that." He reached for the package.

"No, you won't." She clutched the box to her chest, knowing it contained the evidence her sister had mailed home. "Agent Nate Patterson has been waiting for this package. I'll take it to him before I leave post."

"That won't be necessary. From the looks of your car out back and the suitcase in the rear seat, you must be headed home to Alabama."

"But I've got time to stop by Nate's office." She attempted to step around the soldier, but he stopped her forward progression.

She squared her shoulders and glared up at him, hoping to mask her fear. "Is there a problem?" Her voice was firm and laced with more bravado than she felt.

"Now, ma'am, you wouldn't want to delay your trip." He grabbed the box and her hand at the same time.

She tried to jerk free of his hold. "What are you doing?"

"Making sure this box doesn't end up in the wrong place." She tried to scream, but he wrapped his arm around her neck, constricting her airway.

"You...can't...get...away with this," Maggie gasped, fighting to free herself.

"I can and I will."

"Agent Patterson...knows...I'm here."

"Sorry to inform you, ma'am, but the last time I saw him, he was headed off post." Easing up on her throat, he twisted her arm behind her back. "Which is exactly where we're going."

She sucked in a ragged breath. "The neighbors will see you."

He jerked harder on her arm. "In case you didn't notice, the quarters to the right are currently unoccupied, and the major who lives on the left is en route home from Afghanistan. If you think someone will see my car, it's parked in the garage so no one knows I'm even here."

The MP had an answer for everything.

"As soon as I get you taken care of, I'll move your Saturn into the garage and dispose of it later where no one will find it for days. Maybe weeks."

"Dani told me the military police couldn't be trusted."

"Yet it seems you trusted Mr. Patterson."

Maggie jerked at the mention of Nate's name. "Are you saying he's involved?"

Mills laughed. "Patterson's a straight arrow. He plays everything by the book."

"And you're the exact opposite. Whatever you're involved in is despicable. Dani knew something was going on. That's why you killed her."

He shoved Maggie through the kitchen and into the garage. She stumbled, nearly falling. Nearing the military sedan, he opened the trunk. "Climb in."

The thought of being locked in the confined space sent her heart crashing against her chest. "I…I can't."

He raised his hand. "You can and you will, lady." The MP struck her on the side of her skull. She staggered, trying to remain upright.

"Do you know what happens to people who disobey my orders? They end up dead, like the soldier in North Georgia who tried to keep a shipment meant for someone else." A second blow took her breath away. Darkness overshadowed her, and she tumbled forward. The trunk slammed shut, enclosing her like a coffin.

"Nate?" she called out before she floated into oblivion.

Nate's mood was at rock bottom when he drove back to post. Thorndike had been a no-show, and the guy hanging around the Garrett post office left the area before the Postal Inspectors could pick him up for questioning. Nate had hoped the point of contact would shed light on all those involved in the mail scheme and reveal exactly what the packages contained.

In Nate's opinion, drugs ranked at the top of the list of possibilities. Dogs randomly sniffed for illegal substances mailed back to the U.S, but the number of troops in Afghanistan and the high volume of shipments made the odds in favor of the smugglers.

If information had come to light that had bearing on Major Bennett's death being a homicide, Nate would have been able to go to Wilson and make the case for further investigation he now believed it warranted.

In spite of the lack of evidence, Nate needed to contact his boss and ask Wilson to disregard the request for transfer. Now that Maggie had come into his life, Nate wanted more time at Fort Rickman. Independence, Alabama, where she lived, wasn't that far away. He could make the trip in a couple hours.

Needing to hear her voice, he called Maggie's cell. When it went to voice mail, he disconnected and tried Kelly's BOQ landline, surprised when the special agent answered.

"What are you doing back on post?" he asked. "I thought you'd be in North Georgia for a few more days."

"My mother's in the hospital. Wilson told me to take as much time as I need so I'm packing some things before I leave for home."

"I'm sorry about your mom, Kelly."

"Thanks, Nate. She's had medical problems for a long time so it wasn't completely unexpected."

"Did you learn anything new concerning the soldier who died?"

"Only that he gave his girlfriend expensive jewelry. His latest gift had been a large emerald pendant."

"On an E-4's paycheck?"

"Exactly."

"Is Maggie around? I need to talk to her."

"She's gone, Nate, and so is her suitcase. She left a note thanking me for my hospitality."

Nate hung up and tried Maggie's cell once again. Unable to connect, he speed dialed Jamison. "Any word on Thorndike?"

"Negative."

"I'm headed to Hunter Housing Area. I want to talk to Kyle Foglio. Mills questioned the family after Major Bennett's death and learned nothing, yet I wonder if the young man may be holding something back."

"Let me know if you learn anything, Nate. I'll call you as soon as Thorndike contacts us."

"Haul him in for questioning. He was the first on the scene at Major Bennett's murder and at the BOQ after someone had broken in through the back door. He had glass in his boots, although Corporal Mills did, as well. But Thorndike made a point of making excuses for the shards that had dug into his soles. Plus he hovered close when Maggie had picked up a box delivered to Quarters 1448. If Thorndike planned to intercept the shipment, he may have thought Maggie's photo was whatever evidence Major Bennett mailed into the U.S."

"What photo?"

"It's a long story. Just find Thorndike."

Maggie's first indication she was still alive was the roar of raging water, followed by pain. Her head ached as if her skull had shattered into a thousand pieces. Moaning under her breath, she tried to remember what had happened, but her mind refused to focus on anything except the flashes of white lightning that zigzagged through her brain.

She moved slightly, causing her stomach to roil.

Clamping down on her jaw, she tried to calm the internal storm that was assaulting her body, yet her head pounded even more.

A muffled voice filtered through her broken world. She blinked an eye open. A burst of light sent a volley of electric jolts across her temples, forcing her to retreat back into the darkness.

The voice grew louder, and the static of background noise subsided long enough for Maggie to make out bits and pieces of the one-sided conversation. Once again, she forced her eyes open. The MP stood with his back to Maggie, a cell phone at his ear.

"Roger that, sir." She blinked the digital patterned uniform into focus. "She's alive, but out cold. I'll return to post and get rid of her car before I get rid of her."

Maggie's stomach roiled once again. Another wave of vertigo pitched her into blackness, and she heard nothing except distant thunder and rushing water.

Nate parked in front of Quarters 1448 and crossed the street. He held up his identification when Mrs. Foglio opened the door to her quarters. "Mr. Patterson, CID, ma'am. I need to talk to your stepson."

Frustration flashed from her eyes. "Can't you leave him alone?"

"I'm sorry, ma'am, but this is important."

"That's what you people keep saying." She stepped back from the door, allowing Nate to enter the foyer. A television played in the rear of the house.

"Kyle, someone wants to talk to you."

The kid frowned as he lumbered down the hallway. "Yeah?"

Despite the boy's attitude, Nate noticed that he had

removed two of the three studs in his nose, and when he spoke, his tongue was free of metal, as well. Maybe Lieutenant Colonel Foglio and his wife were having a positive influence after all.

"The night Major Bennett committed suicide, did you see anything outside?" Nate asked. "Anything that looked unusual?"

"He was sound asleep," Mrs. Foglio interjected before her stepson could answer. "I was out of town, visiting my sister that night, but my husband talked to the MP who questioned everyone on the block."

Nate held up his hand. "Please, ma'am, I need Kyle to answer."

"My husband said Kyle went to bed early and slept late, Mr. Patterson."

"Ma'am, please." Nate turned his attention to the boy. "Your bedroom is in the front of the house and looks onto the street. What did you see that night?"

Kyle glanced down at the floor then shrugged. "A cop car kept cruising the neighborhood. He probably wanted to make sure I wasn't getting into trouble."

"Were any cars parked near the house, either on the main road or in the alley behind the quarters?"

Kyle wiped the palms of his hands on his jeans. "I snuck out that night to meet a friend."

"Oh, no," the stepmother groaned.

"Go on." Nate held the young man's gaze. "Tell me what happened."

"I cut through the open field behind 1448 on the way home. That's when I saw the MP car parked in the alley."

Nate raised his brow. "The same car that had patrolled the neighborhood earlier?"

"I'm not sure, but the MP came out of Major Bennett's house and drove away."

"What time was that?"

"My girlfriend texted me right afterward." The teen pulled his cell from his pocket and punched a few buttons. "Twelve-forty."

"Did you see anyone else?"

"Yeah. A guy dressed in regular clothes left a little later and walked to a red Mustang. The streetlights were out, and it was pretty dark so I couldn't see his face. All I know is that he was a big guy, like my dad."

"Built?"

Kyle nodded. "Totally."

Nate's gut clenched. Graham Hughes.

"Have you seen either of those two men since then?"

"I think the MP was back today. I saw him after I gave the package to the lady."

Nate's gut tightened. "Which lady?"

"The postman delivered a box that was addressed to 1448," Mrs. Foglio volunteered. "I had Kyle take it across the street. He said Dani's sister answered the door."

"Did you see her leave the house, ma'am?"

"No. But Kyle saw an MP car pull out of the garage about ten minutes later."

Nate's heart exploded in his chest. "Do you still have the key to the quarters?"

Mrs. Foglio must have recognized the urgency in his voice. Without delay, she hurried into the kitchen and returned with the key.

Nate raced across the street and pulled his weapon as he entered the house. A rapid search of the downstairs revealed no changes from the last time he was there, except for the plastic bag, containing the wrapped flag and medals. Taking the stairs two at a time, he checked the bedrooms then threw open the attic door. Fear iced his veins, imagining what he might discover.

Slowly, he climbed the stairs, his eyes searching the rafters. Finding nothing, he let out a ragged breath and retraced his steps. Once in his car, he called Jamison and quickly filled him in on what the Foglio boy had said.

"Send in a team to sweep the quarters for prints. Send a *Be On the Lookout* notice to the Georgia and Alabama Highway Patrols for a silver Saturn and a red Mustang. The MPs should have both license plate numbers in their database."

"Roger that."

"Maggie was right. Graham Hughes came back to the house and parked his Mustang in the alley the night Major Bennett was killed. Thorndike may be involved. Haul both of them in. Search their homes. Search their offices. Go into their computers. Find any information you can that might determine what they've done with Maggie."

SIXTEEN

Jamison met Nate at the door to the CID Headquarters. "No one's seen Graham Hughes. We located the gal from the bar and grill. She said Graham planned to go down to the Gulf Coast for a few days."

"Can she call him on his cell?"

"He's not answering."

"Contact Florida law enforcement. Tell them to locate Graham and bring him back to Fort Rickman."

"Roger that, Nate. What about Wanda?"

"Pull her in. I want to talk to her, as well. Maybe she knows something about Maggie."

A jackhammer pounded in Maggie's head. She grimaced and shifted on the thin mattress where she lay. Glancing around the cabin, she spied a sink, stove and refrigerator in the far corner. Dani's package from Afghanistan sat on a small table nearby.

Licking her dry lips, she longed for a drink of water and an aspirin. Preferably two. She sniffed the damp air that smelled like a musty basement and wondered about the perpetual hum of running water. Attempting to roll to her side, she realized too late that her hands and legs were tied to the bedposts. She yanked at the restraints, but the plastic ties cut into her wrists and held her bound.

"God, please help me."

The rumble of a car engine sent a shiver of apprehension up her spine. She stared at the door, praying it would remain shut while thoughts of Dani and Kendra played through her mind. Had they been killed by the same MP who planned to "get rid of her" as soon as he returned from disposing of her car?

Fear clasped down on her gut and made her want to lash out at anything and anyone. She'd fight to the death, of that she was sure. Then she tried to raise her head and was overcome with a combination of vertigo and nausea.

No matter how strong she wanted to be, she'd been knocked unconscious and had probably suffered a concussion. Her body couldn't regroup to fight off anyone at this point, but at least she could put up a struggle.

Footsteps approached. The doorknob turned. Her pulse went into overdrive, and adrenaline pulsed through her veins, adding more pressure to her head that already threatened to explode.

Maggie closed her eyes, hoping to appear unconscious.

Footsteps scurried across the wooden floor and stopped at the bedside. A hand grabbed her shoulder. "Maggie?"

She recognized the voice.

Opening her eyes, she didn't know whether to scream or rejoice.

"Graham?"

* * *

Nate looked up as Jamison stuck his head through the door to his office. "Thorndike walked in on his own accord. We've got him in interrogation room one."

"Thank God." Nate raced out of his office.

Jamison caught up with him in the hallway. Placing his hand on Nate's arm, the agent cautioned, "Don't lose your cool."

As much as he wanted to pound information out of Thorndike, Jamison was right. Nate needed to stay in control. Rage would only compound the situation.

When he entered the interrogation room, Sergeant Thorndike jumped to his feet. "Sir, what's going on? I had car trouble on the way to Garrett. My cell was out of range so I had to hoof it to Pine City to get help."

"Sit down, Sergeant."

"Not until you tell me why you hauled me in today."

Nate put his knuckles on the table and leaned forward. "I said sit down."

Thorndike fisted his hands. Fire smoldered in his eyes, but he lowered his weighty body into the chair and continued to glare at Nate.

"You were the first on scene for Major Bennett's suicide, is that correct, Sergeant?"

"Yes, sir."

"What about sixteen years ago when Lieutenant Colonel Bennett took his own life? Do you remember being the first on scene that night, as well?"

Thorndike's face clouded. "You think I killed the major?"

"You tell me."

"I didn't do it, sir."

"You knew about her father's death, yet you didn't reveal that information?"

Thorndike hung his head. "Sir, I'll tell you the truth. I didn't make the connection between the two cases until a couple days ago when I was going through some of the awards I've received over the years. Found a picture of me with Colonel Rogers, the provost marshal at that time. I got to thinking about all the cases I'd been involved in and realized Daniel Bennett was the major's father. I was embarrassed about not telling anyone and figured I'd look like a fool coming forth with the information this late in the investigation. Plus I didn't see any reason it would have a bearing on the case. It's been sixteen years, sir."

"You were first on scene when Agent McQueen's BOQ was broken into, isn't that right, Sergeant?"

"Ah, yes, sir."

"The soles of your shoes were crusted with glass."

"Which I brought to your attention."

Thorndike had pulled a number of tours in Iraq but had never served in Afghanistan where the mail ring originated. Still, AmeriWorks, the company Graham Hughes worked for, had contracts in that country. Thorndike could be working with Graham, which would explain how the sergeant's "little woman" afforded to shop in all the high-end boutiques on her frequent trips to Atlanta.

After a volley of rapid-fire questions from Nate, Thorndike shrugged and averted his gaze. "Fact is, sir, my memory's been slipping this past year. Time for me to retire and head south. Get that house the little woman and I have been dreaming about."

Nate needed information, not some excuse about

old age. Before he could ask another question, a knock sounded and the door opened. Jamison motioned to Nate. "I need to see you." Letting out a pent-up lungful of air, Nate joined him in the hallway.

"According to Wanda, someone borrowed Graham Hughes's Mustang the night Major Bennett was killed. Wanda received a large sum of money in return for keeping Graham occupied inside the bar until she got an all clear. By that time, she had decided to take Graham home for the night."

"Did she provide a name?

"Her contact was Wally Turner."

"As in Wally's Pawn?"

"You got that right."

"Notify the FBI. They'll want to talk to Wally as well as a guy named LeShawn and one named Ronald Jones, who goes by Bubba. I mentioned them earlier." Nate hesitated before he asked, "What about Maggie?"

"Wanda doesn't know anything about her, but we'll keep pressing."

In Nate's opinion, that wasn't good enough.

Graham stared down at the restraints holding Maggie bound. His face wore a mix of anger and frustration. The same emotions she was feeling.

She tugged on the ties, trying once again to free herself. "I was right all along, wasn't I, Graham? You killed Dani, but no one believed me."

"No one believed you because it isn't true."

"Maybe you didn't hang her from the rafter, but you planned her death even if you had that military guy do the job."

Graham stepped into the kitchen area and opened one drawer after another. "What military guy?"

"The brute who knocked me out and shoved me into the trunk of his car."

Removing something from the last drawer, Graham returned to her bedside and leaned over Maggie. She could feel his breath on her cheek. Her pulse raced with fear.

"Do you still remember the night we were together down by the river?" he asked.

Her cheeks burned. As if she could forget what happened. When he raised his hand, she saw the butcher knife he held. She had to keep talking to distract him. "You were using me to get back at Dani."

"The truth was I was using Dani to get to you. I told you how I felt, but you never answered my letters. I wrote every week until I finally realized you didn't want anything to do with me." He touched his finger to the blade, checking its sharpness.

She shrunk back. "I...I never received any letters, Graham."

He lowered the knife.

Maggie's heart catapulted against her chest and she tried to backpedal in the bed, knowing in half a heartbeat the razor-sharp blade would cut through her flesh.

Nate needed information no one could provide. If only he could think clearly, but all that came to mind was that Maggie was in danger. When he closed his eyes, he saw her sister's lifeless body hanging from the rafters and Kendra's child, who no longer had a mother to love her. *Come on, Nate. Why can't you pull this case together?*

He opened his eyes to Wanda, who sat across the table from him, crying like a baby.

"Do you have any idea who Wally was working for or who was setting up Graham to be the fall guy by using his Mustang?" Nate asked.

Wanda shook her head. Her face was splotched, her eyes red and swollen. "I thought it was some type of a joke they were playing on him."

Yeah, right. "Is Wally a regular at the bar and grill?"

She blew her nose into a tissue. "He comes in about once a week."

"Who does he talk to?"

"No one. He's a loner." She paused and then held up her hand. "But there's another guy who stops by every so often. Funny last name. Seems to me I saw him with Wally about a month ago."

Nate needed an ID. "What's the guy look like?"

"Kind of nondescript. He's a big guy but not too smart."

"But his last name's unusual?"

"Starts with a Z."

An alert siren went off in Nate's head. "Zart?"

"That's it."

Jamison dashed into the room followed by Corporal Raynard Otis. "One of the choppers from the 5th Aviation Detachment just landed. On the way back to post, they spied something from the air."

Nate followed the two agents into the hallway and listened as Jamison filled him in. "Otis got word they spotted a red Mustang heading south along the River Road."

"Where's that road lead?"

The corporal held up a map. "Eventually to Florida. The river narrows around the bend. There's a rise on the other side where a few fishermen have cabins. The only way across are two somewhat makeshift bridges. The closest is an old, rickety wooden structure. The distant bridge is a bit more stable."

Nate put his hand on Jamison's shoulder. "Contact the Freemont police and State Highway Patrol for help. Tell them that we're looking for Arnold Zart. Call Florida and have them stand by in case he heads that far south."

"What about Graham?" Jamison asked.

"I'm not sure. Zart's got to be involved. He flies in and out of Afghanistan on a regular basis. Easy enough to set up a mail ring while he's in that country, but in my opinion, he's not smart enough to coordinate the whole operation. His desk sits next to Graham's in the contracting office on post so he had access to Graham's keys and could have made a spare for both his quarters on post and his car."

Jamison pulled out his phone. "I'll start contacting the civilian law enforcement agencies."

Nate motioned to the corporal. "Come with me."

With Otis in pursuit, Nate raced to interrogation room one and threw open the door, startling Thorndike. "You fish with a few guys on post. Did Arnold Zart ever join you?"

The sergeant nodded. "A couple of times."

"Didn't you tell me about a cabin south of post on

the opposite side of the river? I need to know how to get there."

Thorndike gave him directions. On his way out the door, Nate yelled at Otis over his shoulder. "Tell Jamison to dispatch a unit to the cabin. Then contact 5th Aviation and tell them to scout out the area from the air."

"Sir, a storm's coming in. All aircraft are grounded."

Nate needed help. "Come on, God. Give me a break."

"Sir?"

"Tell Jamison to use the southern route to the cabin. I'll cross the river at the more northern access."

"But, sir, we got word the water's cresting the bridge. You'll be washed downstream."

"Then pray I can swim, Corporal."

"Yes, sir."

SEVENTEEN

"Someone kept my letters from you, Maggie. Either your mother or Dani."

Confused by what Graham had just said, Maggie watched him cut the ties and free her hands and feet. Grabbing her shoulder, he pulled her up to a sitting position. The room swirled around her. She moaned, overcome with another swell of nausea.

"Are you okay?"

She rubbed her wrists. "Give me a second." The room stabilized, but her thoughts remained jumbled.

Graham had written her?

"You thought I was using you because I'd used other girls. But you were different, Maggie."

"I was just another conquest for you, Graham." She shook her head at her own naïveté. "And to think what almost happened that night."

He let out a ragged breath. "If you hadn't stopped me, we would have had even more to regret."

She looked up, startled. "I…I stopped you? I always thought it was the other way around."

"You said you couldn't do that to Dani. Plus you were a nice girl. That's why I fell for you."

Bile soured Maggie's stomach at the memory of what

she had done. "Nice girls don't go into the woods with their sister's boyfriend. You may have used me, Graham, but I used you to get back at Dani."

Maggie thought of the hateful words Dani had hurled at her, words that cut her to the quick about how their father didn't love her, how Maggie was ugly and timid and she would never have anyone who really cared about her.

If only she had endured Dani's outrage in silence, like she had the other times. Instead she had gone to the party by the river and flaunted herself at Graham. Then she'd followed him into the nearby woods when the other kids weren't watching. The cops eventually closed down the party and took the teens home to their parents. Late that night, Maggie told Dani everything—except that the "other" girl had been Maggie.

Dani hadn't known how to react to Graham's rejection. Their father had been tied up with his own problems and was even more distant than usual. Looking back, Maggie realized Dani had shoplifted in hopes of getting their father's attention. The commanding general called their dad into his office, and the next thing they knew, he'd been relieved of his duties. The following night, their mother found him in the attic.

"My...my mother kept saying over and over again that all the problems had started with me." The shame of what Maggie had done swept over her, filling her with anguish. "When Dani and I met for lunch in Alabama I wanted to tell her the truth and ask her forgiveness."

"She knew."

Tears stung Maggie's eyes. "But she never said anything."

"Dani forgave you long ago, but she didn't know how to ask you to forgive her."

A lump filled Maggie's throat. Graham wrapped his arm around her shoulders and pulled Maggie to her feet. "We need to get out of here. My car's outside."

Steeling herself, she swiped her hand over her cheek and sniffed. "The box." She pointed to where it sat on the table. "Nate needs the evidence."

Grabbing the package with one hand, Graham held her up with the other. With his help, she stumbled forward. He pushed the door open, and she followed him outside, chilled by the wind that gusted through the trees and the light mist that had continued to fall.

"Just a little farther, Maggie."

"How…how did you find me?"

"I knew Dani wouldn't have taken her own life. Someone made her death mirror your father's. There was only one person I had ever confided in about his suicide. Shortly before Dani redeployed home, he came over one night with a bottle of red wine in hand. The alcohol and his leading questions loosened my tongue. We had been together socially a number of times. He seemed like a nice guy, or so I thought. But before long, I had revealed everything. Today when I stopped by the house to pick up some things, I saw your dad's medals and flag in the plastic bag. I knew you wouldn't leave them behind. Then it was just a matter of putting together some of the things I had overheard at work and determining where he had taken you."

"He?"

"The person who masterminded this entire operation that Dani must have stumbled onto in Afghanistan. I realized he had to have been the one who killed her. I just didn't know why. When I went back to the office and checked the AmeriWorks records, everything made sense."

Tires screeched in the distance, causing them both to look toward the road. Graham nudged her forward. "Hurry."

Reaching his Mustang, Maggie leaned against the rear door. Graham dug for the keys in his pocket.

Before he could open the door, a silver Saturn—Maggie's silver Saturn—pulled into the clearing and braked to a stop. The MP who had been on the cell earlier crawled from the passenger side. A second man sat behind the wheel, but his face was hidden by the tinted windows.

Mills pulled his weapon.

Graham pushed Maggie to the ground and gunfire exploded around them. Something warm and wet spread across her back as Graham's full weight fell momentarily upon her shoulders. The package from Afghanistan had taken a hit and shattered into scraps of shredded cardboard and broken earthenware.

Struggling to rise, Maggie put one hand on the car door and reached for Graham with the other. As if in slow motion, his hand slipped out of her grasp. When she looked down, all she could see was the gaping hole in his chest and the precious gems scattered around his body from the broken package.

Another burst of gunfire caused her to turn. The MP fell across the hood of her car, and the driver lay slumped over the wheel.

Whimpering, she watched the shooter step into the clearing. He aimed a gun straight at her heart. "You and I need to take a little walk down to the river."

* * *

Nate headed south out of post along the narrow, two-lane road that wound through the countryside. Usually the trip was relaxing, but today, with the steady stream of rain and the strong wind adding to his worry over Maggie, conditions were less than ideal. As far as Nate knew only a handful of folks lived on this side of post, and many of them had evacuated the area due to the rising water.

Common sense told him to bypass the first bridge and head for the more stable southern access, but he went with his gut instinct that kept screaming Maggie was in danger and he needed to find her fast. Besides, if Zart had made it to the other side, Nate would, as well.

An isolated fishing cabin would be the ideal spot to hold her hostage. Nate shook his head and groaned. He should have listened to Maggie. She'd been convinced her sister had been murdered, but Nate had been too focused on evidence that never materialized.

Eight months ago, he had made a mistake by allowing his brother to sway his opinion, which had cost Michael his life. Nate had become too cautious so he'd closed his mind to what Maggie offered as a logical explanation.

The rain intensified, making it difficult to see the road. Nate clamped his hands around the steering wheel—white-knuckled, struggling against the powerful wind that threatened to push the car off the narrow roadway.

The bridge appeared in the distance. Corporal Otis had been right about the rickety structure. The crossing had been constructed years ago without side guardrails. If only the aged wood could withstand the pressure from the driving water long enough for Nate to make it to the other side.

A momentary lull in the storm cleared his view. He spied the cabin huddled close to the water's edge. A blur of metallic red was visible through the underbrush.

Graham's Mustang.

Nate picked up his cell phone and pushed the speed dial for Jamison. "I'm approaching the bridge. Water's spilling over the sides, but it looks navigable. I've got a visual on the red Mustang parked in the underbrush near the cabin. I'm moving in."

"The bridge from the south is washed out, Nate. We won't be able to get to you."

"What about from the air?"

"Not in this storm."

"Then I'll have to handle this one on my own."

When Jamison failed to respond, Nate glanced at his cell. *Call Disconnected.* No bars. No reception. He threw his phone on the passenger seat, knowing he couldn't rely on anyone else for help.

Anyone except the Lord.

Pulling in a ragged breath, he gripped the steering wheel even harder. "I don't deserve Your help, God, but Maggie does. Let's work together to save her."

The bridge lay ahead. Water washed over the wooden planks. Nate shifted into low gear and eased the car onto the bridge, keeping an even pressure on the accelerator. If the engine died, he'd have to risk hoofing it to the other side. Feeling the pull of the water, Nate knew he'd be sucked into the river and washed downstream.

"Stay with me, Lord," he muttered. Without railings, he could be headed off the bridge and straight into the swirling mass of water. Once the wheels gripped pavement on the far side, he let out a sigh of relief. Maybe God was listening after all.

Increasing his speed, Nate approached the cabin and parked in the underbrush, knowing surprise would be an advantage. He pulled his weapon from his holster, grateful for the sound of the rushing water and the rumble of thunder that muffled his footsteps. Two cars sat in the clearing. Rounding the Mustang, his heart leaped to his throat.

Graham lay on the ground, the broken shards of earthenware and the remains of a shipment box still in his hand. His gut hung open, and blood, mixed with rainwater, pooled around his ashen body. The mail ring hadn't been about drugs, but precious gems like the stones scattered in the debris.

Maggie's Saturn was parked nearby. A second victim lay slumped over the hood. Blood oozed from the back of his head. Nate turned the body over and groaned. Corporal Mills stared back at him with a bullet hole between his eyes.

Flicking his gaze around the clearing, Nate stepped to the driver's side, keeping his gun raised and his senses on high alert. He opened the door and, using his free hand, lifted the third victim's shoulder until he could make an ID. Arnold Zart.

Nate's neck prickled. A noise made him turn. Footsteps broke through the underbrush along a path that led to the water's edge.

Knowing Kendra's body had been pulled from the river, Nate's gut constricted. *Oh, dear, God, no. Not Maggie.*

EIGHTEEN

Lieutenant Colonel Foglio stepped into the clearing. Nate saw a flash of steel and heard the bullet fire immediately after he got off the first round.

Hot, searing pain cut through his left upper arm. Nate gasped, firing another round that caught Foglio in the chest. He crumbled onto one knee.

Racing forward, Nate grabbed Foglio's lapels and raised him off the ground. "What have you done with her?"

The officer shook his head. "She's gone."

Nate shook him again. "Tell me."

"The water. The last I saw she was headed downstream." He tried to laugh, but choked on the blood that gurgled in his throat.

Nate threw him down on the ground and kicked his gun into the underbrush. Foglio might survive, but he wouldn't leave the area on his own accord.

Determined to find Maggie, Nate ran along the path. The bushes pulled at his clothes. He shrugged out of his jacket and dropped his gun on the ground near the water's edge. Toeing out of his shoes, he scanned the wide expanse of river. A sea of dark, churning water raced south. Running in the direction of the flow, Nate searched for any sign of her.

"Maggie," he screamed, knowing she'd never hear him over the river's fury.

A huge pine tree, uprooted by the rain, lay half submerged in the water. Its branches had formed a makeshift dam.

A splash of orange caught his eye.

Maggie!

Nate dove into the river. The cold took his breath away. He came up gasping for air, unable to orient himself. Finally he saw her hung up in the downed foliage.

The current propelled him forward. He neared the pine and grabbed one of the branches that broke before he could establish a firm hold. Kicking with all his might, Nate steered his body closer to where the current had entwined her among the boughs. Her eyes were closed, but her head was above water.

"Maggie," he screamed again.

Her eyes opened. She flailed. The motion caused the pine to shift. Nate caught her just as the tree groaned and released her from its hold. He pulled her close and encircled her with his good arm.

"Feetfirst," he screamed, turning her so her face would be protected from any obstacle floating in the water.

His fingers tightened on her shoulder. *God, don't let me lose her now.*

Lightning illuminated the darkening sky, and thunder cracked overhead. If the river didn't kill them, the storm could.

"Keep your legs up, Maggie. Watch out for rocks and floating debris."

The water sped them along like a kayak on rapids. Waves broke over them, spewing brown water, thick with mud, into their eyes and mouth. Maggie coughed, once again flailing. The motion turned them about-face and prevented Nate from seeing what lay ahead. He kicked his legs, grateful when they reversed position.

Growing intensely fatigued, Nate lifted his left arm out of the water. His raw flesh oozed red. He hadn't realized how much blood he was losing. Continuing at the present rate would be his undoing.

Please, God.

Up ahead, a portion of a boat dock had broken free and was jammed between two boulders, forming an oasis in the middle of the swirling river.

"Aim for the platform." Nate kicked and forced Maggie forward. She grabbed the edge of the wooden barrier and held on tight. Her face was too pale, and she shivered in the frigid water. She wouldn't last much longer. Land was too far away, and the current too strong for them to swim to shore.

Nate encircled Maggie with his arms, hoping his body heat would warm her. If only she could crawl onto the dock. "Honey, try to shimmy up onto the wood."

Maggie struggled to raise herself, and with Nate's help, she eventually collapsed onto the platform, gasping for air.

"Now you, Nate." She reached for his hand.

"I...I'm okay in the water." He could barely hold on to the side of the dock. His feet were being yanked under by the current, and he no longer had the energy to withstand the strong pull.

So many things swirled through his head that he wanted to tell her about her dad and how she wasn't to blame for his death. Hopefully, Colonel Rogers would reveal all that if she ever made it to safety.

Then he mentally corrected himself. *When* she made it to safety. *Please, Lord, make it happen.*

Nate's face was white as death and blood seeped from the wound on his shoulder. Maggie tried to pull him onto the platform, but she lacked the strength to do so, and he was too exhausted to help.

"You…you were right, Maggie, about your sister's death. I should have listened to you from the beginning."

"Shh, Nate." She put her finger to his lips. "Don't waste your energy. It doesn't matter now. At least I know Dani didn't take her own life."

"You're…you're not to blame for your father's death, either." Nate's eyes closed.

She grabbed his good shoulder. "Help will be here soon. Don't leave me, Nate."

The frigid temperature and loss of blood were sapping the life from him. She lowered herself into the water and cradled him in her arms.

"God brought us together for a reason. I'm not going to let you go." But as the sun began to set over the horizon and the temperature dipped even lower, Maggie began to fear that neither she nor Nate would live to see the dawn of a new day.

NINETEEN

Maggie had to remain strong. Nate was depending on her. The rain subsided, and the clouds parted bringing the last rays of the evening sun to shine down on them as if the Lord were touching them with His light.

Maggie turned her face toward the sky, hoping to feel warmth from the setting sun. She didn't feel anything except the cold wind, but she heard a sound that stirred her heart.

Searching the sky, she saw a tiny pinpoint of black in the distance. The spot grew closer and brought with it the *whomp, whomp, whomp* of a helicopter flying overhead.

"Nate!" She shook him and pointed to the heavens. "Look. They found us."

Despite the hypothermia that had settled over him, he smiled. Maggie waved her arm in the air. She felt a surge of elation when the chopper hovered above the water and dropped a harness down to them.

Nate grabbed for the straps. "Fasten…these…around you," he said through tight lips.

Once the harness was securely around her chest, Maggie reached out for him. "Hold on to me, Nate. We'll go up together."

"You'll…you'll never make it with me hanging on." He raised his hand, signaling the crew in the craft. The harness started to rise, taking her from him.

"No," she screamed. Nate wouldn't survive long enough for the crew to lower the harness again. "Grab my hand. We'll do this together."

"I…I can't."

"You saved me, Nate. Now let me save you."

She opened her arms.

He reached for Maggie, and she pulled him close. He straddled the harness with her in it, and together they were lifted into the air.

The crew pulled them into the chopper. Maggie collapsed onto the floor of the craft next to Nate. She reached for his cold hand and entwined her fingers through his.

"We made it, Nate." Looking into his lifeless eyes, Maggie realized the truth. They may have made it to safety, but it might not be in time for Nate.

Maggie left her hospital room, in spite of the doctor's orders to remain in bed. She had to see for herself.

A team of specialists had been waiting when the chopper landed at the military hospital on post. Nate's condition had been touch and go throughout the night. While in the O.R., he had received four units of blood, and although the wound on his shoulder had been stitched up, infection was the biggest concern. Round-the-clock IV antibiotics were working to stave off the virulent organisms that had spiked his temperature and threatened to shut down his major organs. Although Nate still wasn't in the clear, the last report had been more favorable.

Maggie was taking oral antibiotics and had been watched closely after a CAT scan revealed a severe concussion. Her vital signs were good, but not good enough to be walking around the hospital.

Finding Nate's room, she pushed through the door and stepped to his bedside. A wave of anxiety passed through her when she gazed down at his ashen face. Unable to keep her hands to herself, she reached out and touched his cheek, surprised to see his eyes flutter open.

"Maggie."

She smiled, feeling her heart swell with emotion.

"How…are…you?" he asked through cracked lips.

"Fine, now that I'm with you." Her eyes clouded as she thought of what could have happened. "For a moment there, I didn't think you wanted to go with me into the chopper."

His lips curled into a weak smile. "That was hypothermia talking."

A knock sounded at the door. Maggie turned in time to see Jamison and Chief Wilson step into the room. "The nurse told us you were both doing better," the chief said as the two men moved to the bed and smiled down at Nate. "Proves a good CID agent can withstand just about anything, even a raging river."

"The doctors weren't very optimistic when they brought him in last night," Maggie reminded them. Both men had been there when the helicopter had touched down and had stayed until morning.

The chief's upbeat expression sobered. "We were all worried about you, Nate. You went above and beyond on this one."

"Thank you, sir."

"I'm sure you're interested in what happened," the chief continued. "Foglio confessed to murdering Major Bennett."

"With Corporal Mills's help," Jamison added.

"Did you find out what happened in Afghanistan?" Maggie asked.

"Seems the driver killed in the IED explosion suspected his roommate was involved in a mail ring," Jamison said. "He took one of the earthenware figurines to your sister, Maggie, and asked her what he should do. She convinced him to go to Captain York, the company commander, with the information, and since she wasn't sure who was involved on that end, she mailed the evidence back to the U.S."

The chief nodded. "The roommate must have realized they were on to him. CID in Afghanistan called and told us he confessed to setting the IED that killed the company commander and the soldier."

"And the guys from the pawnshop?" Nate asked, his voice somewhat stronger.

"They've been arrested," Jamison said. "Evidently Graham pawned a gun some time ago that Foglio planned to use on Major Bennett if the copycat suicide didn't work. He borrowed Graham's Mustang, knowing if murder was suspected and if anyone saw the car the night of Major Bennett's death, they'd pin the crime on Graham."

"Then he used the gun on Corporal Mills and Arnold Zart," Nate added.

"Exactly." Jamison nodded. "In his twisted mind, Lieutenant Colonel Foglio thought Graham would be charged with their deaths while he walked away without anyone suspecting his involvement."

Maggie sighed. "I'm just relieved it's over."

The chief glanced at his watch. "We need to get back to the office, but I'll pass on the good news that you're doing better." The men headed for the door and then the chief stopped short. "Oh, I almost forgot. I tore up your paperwork for transfer, Nate."

With a broad smile and a final wave, the chief left the room. Jamison gave his friend a thumbs-up before he followed Wilson out the door.

Maggie turned back to Nate, almost afraid to ask. "Paperwork?"

He squeezed her hand. "I had wanted to go back to Afghanistan before I met you, Maggie. But all that has changed."

"So you're not going to be deployed?"

"I'm staying at Fort Rickman." A smile pulled at the corners of his cracked lips. "Although I plan on spending a lot of time in Alabama."

Her heart skipped a beat. "Sounds like a great idea to me."

He lowered his gaze for a moment. When he looked up at her, his face was serious. "I heard the family counseling office on post has a vacancy."

She didn't need to think about her answer. "Now that's an opportunity I wouldn't want to pass up."

Nate's eyes twinkled. "I was hoping you'd say that."

Knowing there was more information he needed to hear, Maggie said, "Colonel Rogers paid me a visit this morning and told me the truth about my dad. Now I know what you were trying to explain while we were in the water. Dani wasn't to blame for our father's death. Neither was I."

She paused before adding, "For a long time as a

kid, I was jealous of my sister. She seemed to have everything I wanted—a group of friends and a guy who liked her and, on rare occasions, even attention from my dad. I told myself none of that was important to me, but of course, it was. I made a number of mistakes, trying to have what was hers, never realizing love comes to different people in different ways and at different times."

Nate rubbed his fingers over Maggie's hand. "When I was in the recovery room, I asked the Lord to forgive any mistake of mine that had bearing on Michael's death."

"I'm so glad, Nate."

"This morning, I called my parents. My mom started crying when she heard I was in the hospital. She said she knew I wasn't to blame. I didn't know if my father would be as forgiving."

Nate licked his lips before he continued. "My dad…" He hesitated a long moment. "My dad said he was proud of me."

"What's that tell you?" Maggie asked.

"That I don't have to run away from the past."

She leaned over him and took pleasure in seeing the spark of interest light up his eyes. "Not only are you an excellent CID agent, Nate Patterson, but you're also a fast learner." She smiled playfully. "Guess what?"

His lips twitched into a smile. "I don't know, what?"

"I'm proud of you, too." Then Maggie did what she had wanted to do for a very long time. She lowered her lips to his. Despite the IV, he wrapped his good arm around her waist and drew her close. Her last thought as she sank into his embrace was that she would have waited a lifetime to find Nate.

EPILOGUE

Nate pulled his car to the curb. Rounding to the passenger side, he opened the door for Maggie. She stepped to the sidewalk and looked at the one-story brick quarters. A bed of flowers edged the porch—bright red geraniums and white begonias interspersed with bushes of blue hydrangeas.

Maggie nodded her approval. "Nice curb appeal."

"It's not Hunter Housing Area, but we can move in as soon as we get back from our honeymoon."

She squeezed his hand. "It's a wonderful house, Nate, and it's ours."

He wrapped his arm around her waist. "Until Uncle Sam moves me to a new assignment."

"The counseling service on post said they'd transfer me to your next duty station when you get orders."

"They don't want to lose someone as empathetic as you."

"You're biased."

He nuzzled her cheek, making her laugh. "You bet I am."

Wrapping his arm around her, they walked toward their new quarters. "How's Kyle Foglio doing?"

"He still refuses counseling, but he and his stepmom

are talking and that's important. I told Kyle he wasn't to blame for his father's actions."

"Did he believe you?"

"I don't think so. He's leaving in a few days to spend the rest of the summer with his mom."

"And Mrs. Foglio?"

"She's adjusting to civilian life, although she doesn't talk about her husband. Maybe with time, she'll be more forthcoming."

"Must be hard to live for years with someone and not really know them."

Maggie nodded. "I'm beginning to believe all families have secrets. Some are more painful than others."

Nate slipped the key into the lock and pushed the door open. "This time we walk in together." He winked. "Next time, I carry you."

Stepping into the cool interior, he closed the door and took her in his arms. Without a doubt, Maggie was the best thing that had ever happened to him. "Every night before I go to sleep I thank God for bringing you into my life."

Her eyes filled with tears of joy, and laughter bubbled from her throat. "Then He's getting two thank-yous, because I do the same thing."

"Two peas in a pod, eh? Maybe we need to make this permanent."

She gently slapped his shoulder. Although his wound had healed, he still had residual pain. "In exactly two weeks and three days, it will be permanent."

"Hard to believe, isn't it?" He felt his gut tighten, this time not with fear or anxiety, but with overwhelming love for Maggie. Pure, wondrous love that was warm as the summer sunshine and better than anything he'd ever known.

"I love you, Maggie."

"Oh, Nate, I love you so much."

"Promise…" He hesitated, soaking in the feel of her in his arms. "Promise you'll love me forever?"

"Longer than forever." As he lowered his lips to hers, he thought of the journey they had traveled. Both of them had carried heavy burdens from the past that, at the time, had seemed insurmountable. Now, holding the woman he loved more than anything, Nate vowed to enjoy this moment and every moment God gave them, knowing the Lord had a wonderful future planned for their lifetime together.

* * * * *

Dear Reader,

I'm excited about *The Officer's Secret,* the first book in my new Military Investigations Series, which features heroes and heroines in the U.S. Army Criminal Investigation Division. I hope you will enjoy reading this story as much as I enjoyed writing it.

In *The Officer's Secret,* Army CID Special Agent Nate Patterson and family counselor Maggie Bennett butt heads and hearts as they try to uncover the truth about Maggie's family, her sister's mysterious death and an earthenware figurine from Afghanistan that may have been smuggled into the U.S. Like many of us, Maggie and Nate hold on to secrets from the past that keep them from moving forward. Jesus tells us in John's gospel, "The truth will set you free." My fictional heroes need to learn that lesson just as many of us must realize it, as well. Christ wants us to live in His truth and to accept His unconditional love and forgiveness. Only then can we be truly free.

To join my Cross My Heart Prayer Team or to learn about my upcoming books, go to my website, www.DebbyGiusti.com, or my blog, www.crossmyheartprayerteam.blogspot.com.

Wishing you abundant blessings,

Debby Giusti

QUESTIONS FOR DISCUSSION

1. Why did Dani and Maggie both believe they were responsible for their father's death?

2. Did you learn anything new about military life by reading this book?

3. What type of relationship do you think Maggie had with her mother? What about Dani?

4. What did Maggie need as a child that she didn't receive from her family? How did that influence her in adulthood?

5. Was Dani and Graham's marriage flawed from the start? What could they have done to strengthen their relationship?

6. Compare and contrast Nate's family to Maggie's. Which character had a stronger foundation of love and acceptance?

7. Why did Nate feel responsible for his brother's death? What did he need to realize?

8. Do you think Dani had forgiven Maggie?

9. What will happen to Kyle Foglio?

10. What is the significance of the marked scripture passage in Dani's Bible?

11. Did Graham love Dani? What about Maggie?

12. How was Maggie able to take the pain she had experienced as a child and use it to help others in her counseling?

13. How many secrets were revealed in this book?

14. What did Nate learn from Maggie? What did Maggie learn from Nate?

15. Did the truth set Maggie and Nate free?

INSPIRATIONAL

Inspirational romances to warm your heart & soul.

Love Inspired
SUSPENSE

TITLES AVAILABLE NEXT MONTH

Available June 14, 2011

PROTECTING HER OWN
Guardians, Inc.
Margaret Daley

OUT OF TIME
Texas Ranger Justice
Shirlee McCoy

LAWMAN-IN-CHARGE
Laura Scott

BEHIND THE BADGE
Susan Sleeman

LISCNM0511

REQUEST YOUR FREE BOOKS!

2 FREE RIVETING INSPIRATIONAL NOVELS
PLUS 2 FREE MYSTERY GIFTS

Love Inspired®
SUSPENSE

YES! Please send me 2 FREE Love Inspired® Suspense novels and my 2 FREE mystery gifts (gifts are worth about $10). After receiving them, if I don't wish to receive any more books, I can return the shipping statement marked "cancel." If I don't cancel, I will receive 4 brand-new novels every month and be billed just $4.24 per book in the U.S. or $4.74 per book in Canada. That's a saving of at least 23% off the cover price. It's quite a bargain! Shipping and handling is just 50¢ per book in the U.S. and 75¢ per book in Canada.* I understand that accepting the 2 free books and gifts places me under no obligation to buy anything. I can always return a shipment and cancel at any time. Even if I never buy another book, the two free books and gifts are mine to keep forever.

123/323 IDN FDCT

Name	(PLEASE PRINT)	
Address		Apt. #
City	State/Prov.	Zip/Postal Code

Signature (if under 18, a parent or guardian must sign)

Mail to the **Reader Service**:
IN U.S.A.: P.O. Box 1867, Buffalo, NY 14240-1867
IN CANADA: P.O. Box 609, Fort Erie, Ontario L2A 5X3

Not valid for current subscribers to Love Inspired Suspense books.

**Are you a subscriber to Love Inspired Suspense
and want to receive the larger-print edition?
Call 1-800-873-8635 or visit www.ReaderService.com.**

* Terms and prices subject to change without notice. Prices do not include applicable taxes. Sales tax applicable in N.Y. Canadian residents will be charged applicable taxes. Offer not valid in Quebec. This offer is limited to one order per household. All orders subject to credit approval. Credit or debit balances in a customer's account(s) may be offset by any other outstanding balance owed by or to the customer. Please allow 4 to 6 weeks for delivery. Offer available while quantities last.

Your Privacy—The Reader Service is committed to protecting your privacy. Our Privacy Policy is available online at www.ReaderService.com or upon request from the Reader Service.

We make a portion of our mailing list available to reputable third parties that offer products we believe may interest you. If you prefer that we not exchange your name with third parties, or if you wish to clarify or modify your communication preferences, please visit us at www.ReaderService.com/consumerschoice or write to us at Reader Service Preference Service, P.O. Box 9062, Buffalo, NY 14269. Include your complete name and address.

LISUS11

With time running out to stop the Lions of Texas from orchestrating their evil plan, Texas Ranger Levi McDonall must work with his childhood friend to solve his captain's murder and thwart the group's disastrous plot. Read on for a preview of OUT OF TIME by Shirlee McCoy, the exciting conclusion to the TEXAS RANGER JUSTICE series.

Silence told its own story, and Susannah Jorgenson listened as she hurried across the bridge that led to the Alamo Chapel. Darkness had fallen hours ago and the air held a hint of rain. The shadows seemed deeper than usual, the darkness just a little blacker. Or maybe it was simply her imagination that made the Alamo complex seem so forbidding.

She shivered. Not from the cold. Not from the chilly breeze. From the darkness, the silence, the endless echo of her fear as she made her final rounds. She jogged to the chapel and flashed the beam of her light along the corners of the building.

Nothing.

No movement, no sounds, no reason to think she wasn't alone, but she couldn't shake the feeling that she was being watched. That somewhere beyond the beam of her light, danger waited. She did a full sweep of the chapel and of the office area beyond. Nothing, of course.

She opened the chapel door, stepping straight into a broad, muscular chest. Someone grabbed her upper arms, holding her in place.

She shoved forward into her attacker, pushing her weight into a solid wall of strength as she tried to unbalance him.

"Calm down. I was just trying to keep you from falling." The man released his hold.

"Sorry about that. I wasn't expecting anyone to be standing near the door. We're closed for the day, but we'll be open again at seven tomorrow morning." She cleared her throat.

"No need to apologize. I'm Ranger Levi McDonall. My captain said he was going to call and let you know I was on the way."

"Levi McDonall?" Her childhood idol? Her best guy friend? Her first teenage crush?

No way could they be the same.

"Come on in." She hurried into the chapel, trying to pull herself together. This was the Texas Ranger she'd be working with for the next eight days?

She flipped on a light, turned to face McDonall.

Levi McDonall.

Her Levi McDonall.

Can Levi and Susannah put the past behind them to save San Antonio's future? Find out in OUT OF TIME by Shirlee McCoy from Love Inspired Suspense, available in June wherever books are sold.

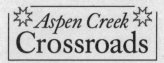
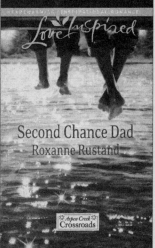